Acting Edition

Feeding Beatrice

A Gothic Tale

by Kirsten Greenidge

⑅SAMUEL FRENCH⑅

ISBN 978-0-573-70938-8

www.concordtheatricals.com
www.concordtheatricals.co.uk

FOR PRODUCTION INQUIRIES

UNITED STATES AND CANADA
info@concordtheatricals.com
1-866-979-0447

UNITED KINGDOM AND EUROPE
licensing@concordtheatricals.co.uk
020-7054-7298

Each title is subject to availability from Concord Theatricals Corp.,
depending upon country of performance. Please be aware that
FEEDING BEATRICE may not be licensed by Concord Theatricals
Corp. in your territory. Professional and amateur producers should
contact the nearest Concord Theatricals Corp. office or licensing
partner to verify availability.

This work is published by Samuel French, an imprint of Concord
Theatricals Corp.

No one shall make any changes in this title(s) for the purpose of production. No part of this book may be reproduced, stored in a retrieval system, scanned, uploaded, or transmitted in any form, by any means, now known or yet to be invented, including mechanical, electronic, digital, photocopying, recording, videotaping, or otherwise, without the prior written permission of the publisher. No one shall share this title(s), or any part of this title(s), through any social media or file hosting websites.

For all inquiries regarding motion picture, television, online/digital and other media rights, please contact Concord Theatricals Corp.

MUSIC AND THIRD-PARTY MATERIALS USE NOTE

Licensees are solely responsible for obtaining formal written permission from copyright owners to use copyrighted music and/or other copyrighted third-party materials (e.g., artworks, logos) in the performance of this play and are strongly cautioned to do so. If no such permission is obtained by the licensee, then the licensee must use only original music and materials that the licensee owns and controls. Licensees are solely responsible and liable for clearances of all third-party copyrighted materials, including without limitation music, and shall indemnify the copyright owners of the play(s) and their licensing agent, Concord Theatricals Corp., against any costs, expenses, losses and liabilities arising from the use of such copyrighted third-party materials by licensees. For music, please contact the appropriate music licensing authority in your territory for the rights to any incidental music.

IMPORTANT BILLING AND CREDIT REQUIREMENTS

If you have obtained performance rights to this title, please refer to your licensing agreement for important billing and credit requirements.

FEEDING BEATRICE was first presented as a staged reading during the University of Iowa's New Works Festival at the University of Iowa in May 2000. It was also presented as a staged reading during the Boston Women On Top Festival in March 2001. It was awarded the Richard Maibaum Award by the University of Iowa in May 2000, as well as second place for the Kennedy Center/American College Theatre Festival's Lorraine Hansberry Award, and second place for the Kennedy Center/American College Theatre Festival's Mark David Cohen Award, also in 2000.

FEEDING BEATRICE premiered on November 23, 2019 at the Repertory Theatre of St. Louis (Hana Sharif, Artistic Director) in Webster Groves, Missouri. The performance was directed by Daniel Bryant, with sets by Lawrence Moteri, costumes by Mika Eubanks, lights by Jason Lynch, sound by David Samba, choregraphy by Heather Beal, and assistant direction by Alexis Cabrera. The stage manager was Shannon B. Sturgis. The cast was as follows:

JUNE	Lorene Chesley
LURIE	Nathan James
LEROY	Ronald Emile
BEATRICE	Allison Winn

FEEDING BEATRICE was presented as a radio play as part of Geva Theatre Center's Recognition Radio series (Mark Cuddy, Artistic Director) starting on October 27, 2020. The performance was directed by Daniel Bryant, with sound by David Samba, dramaturgy by Francisca Da Silveira, and the intern/assistant to the playwright was Charlotte Weinman. The stage manager was Dee Daniels-Koster. The cast was as follows:

JUNE	Lorene Chesley
LURIE	Nathan James
LEROY	Ronald Emile
BEATRICE	Allison Winn

CHARACTERS

JUNE WALKER – a home owner in her mid-thirties, Lurie's wife
LURIE WALKER – a home owner in his mid-thirties, June's husband
LEROY WALKER – Lurie's younger brother, in his early to mid-thirties
BEATRICE – a guest

SETTING

An old house in need of repair in a suburb of Boston, Massachusetts.

TIME

The present.

NOTES ON THE TEXT

Dialogue marked with a slash (/) indicates where overlapping occurs.

Gothic: relating to a genre or style that is characterized or contains a gloomy setting, grotesque, mysterious, or violent events, as well as a culture of degeneration and decay...

ACKNOWLEDGEMENTS

Years ago, I sat in an adaptation class with gifted educator and playwright Naomi Iizuka. To say this course was transformative for me, and for several of my classmates, would be an understatement. Naomi taught us to dream big. She taught us to pay attention to details. She taught us how to take our work seriously without dragging our human selves into the mire of seriousness that sometimes makes that work more difficult that it needs to be. To Naomi, I am eternally grateful for her support and inspiration for this play and the others I began when I was her student.

Feeding Beatrice received much developmental support throughout my last bit of time at the Playwrights' Workshop at Iowa, I am thankful for the keen eye of Maggie Conroy who helped shaped early versions of this work over playwright-director meetings at her and her husband, Frank Conroy's home.

It takes many people to write a play. There are those talks with directors, but also fellow writers, who know the joy and pain of writing and rewriting and rehearsing and then again rewriting, over and over again. While at Iowa, I was fortunate to have the crucial support and warm friendship of some of the loveliest and talented playwrights I know. No matter where my writing life takes me, they will always occupy rooms in my metaphysical artistic home. They are Bronwen Bitetti, Jeanine Columbe, Kara Hartzler, Joe Hiatt, Allison Moore, Tory Stewart, Robert Wray, and David Adjmi. Thank you for all the Monday Workshop nights spent.

Thank you to the Kennedy Center/American College Theatre Festival and its Artistic Director Gregg Henry, who believed not only in this play, but also in me as an artist and in the plays that followed.

As this play became my MFA thesis, I naturally sent it out to many, many theatres and development opportunities, from which the play was often ultimately rejected for production. There was one such organization, however, that sent encouraging words of support along with said rejection, and which kept the play close at hand. Dramaturg Gavin Witt and Hana Sharif, both on staff at Baltimore Center Stage at the time, became champions of the play, and for that I am eternally grateful.

As Artistic Director of Repertory Theatre of St. Louis – one of just a handful of women of color Artistic Directors in this country – Hana Sharif fulfilled her promise that if ever she ran a theatre, *Feeding Beatrice* would be one of the first plays produced. For that I am exceedingly grateful. That Hana paired this play with director Daniel Bryant (also a former staff member at Baltimore Center Stage) has imprinted my artistic life indelibly. Thank you, Daniel, for your keen mind, your deft direction, and your grace when running a rehearsal room so that it feels like a warm embrace of love, work, creativity, and pride. To our cast on that and our subsequent production when *Feeding Beatrice* was presented as a radio play – Lorene Chesley, Nathan James, Ronald Emile, and Allison Winn, thank you, thank you for embodying these characters in ways I imagined and breathing life into them in ways that stretch far beyond anything I had ever thought possible when writing in my apartment in Iowa City.

Thank you also to playwright and dramaturg Francisca Da Silviera who brought *Feeding Beatrice* to the attention of Geva Theatre Center, and to the staff and team who supported this play as we forged it into its audio version.

Without the guidance and expertise of Mark Orsini at Bret Adams, I would be putty. Thank you Mark, Bonnie Davis, and Bruce Ostler for all your work over the span of what is now many years.

And, thank you as always to my friends and family who stand alongside and behind whenever I sit down to write or need to stand up to dance when the writing isn't working or need to text at random throughout the day to remind that we are not alone: Emily Morris, Cayetana Navarro, Charlie Linshaw, Kristin Leahey, Adam Kassim, and Robert Najarian: you have each been in attendance more than you know.

Lastly, thanks to Ariel Dance Greenidge, Kerri Greenidge, Kaitlyn Greenidge, Mavis Ariel Hoyt, Katia Nigro, Hunter Nigro, and Ron Nigro – we all believe in ghosts; I am full of joy and gratitude that I get to discuss them with you all every day so they do not haunt, but instead co-exist.

(While the house lights are still on we hear a loud creaking noise: the sound of an old house settling.)

(The house lights go down.)

(And the creaking stops.)

(A few tinny notes of a music box can be heard.)

(Then.)

(Silence.)

(Light come up on a bathtub.)

(The fingers of two hands curl slowly and deliberately over the rim of the tub.)

(A head rises up...then dips below the tub's rim.)

(Lights lower.)

(The sound of breathing rises, rises, rises in the dark...)

(Lights come up fully on the bathroom, which is a mix of styles from this century and last.)

*(**JUNE** and **LURIE** placing their clothes back on.)*

LURIE. You want lunch?

JUNE. Now every room's been christened.

(LURIE grins at JUNE.)

LURIE. Not the pantry.

JUNE. Yes the pantry. Last Tuesday.

LURIE. Oh yeah.

JUNE. Forgot already?

LURIE. No, I remember.

(He grins.)

Kinda. Maybe I need help to remember *exactly*.

JUNE. Oh yeah?

LURIE. You could show me now, Mrs. Walker, if you want.

JUNE. I just might, Mr. Walker, if I want.

LURIE. "Mr. and Mrs. Walker." Never gets old.

JUNE. And what I would be reminding you, is how we christened that pantry –

LURIE. – Yeah, I definitely need help –

JUNE. *Last Tuesday.*

(They kiss. Quick.)

LURIE. For real, let's get something to eat.

JUNE. We could walk to that place in town. The new little –

LURIE. No, no. I'm in the mood for meat. Like. Like a roast.

JUNE. It looked cute, that little place.

LURIE. I'll go to the market, buy a roast, pick up the paper on the way back.

JUNE. You and that paper. There's these things called phones, they're all the rage.

LURIE. We skipped breakfast. A nice lunch would be –

JUNE. Come back.

> (**JUNE** *wiggles her fingers at* **LURIE.**)

> (**LURIE** *looks at* **JUNE**'*s fingers.*)

> (**LURIE** *looks at* **JUNE** *more fully.*)

Come lie here with me and listen to our house. Come listen to our new home.

> (**JUNE** *wiggles her fingers and cocks her head to the side.*)

> (**LURIE** *smiles.*)

> (**LURIE** *goes to the tub.*)

> (**LURIE** *slides into the tub with* **JUNE.**)

> (*But now.*)

> (*Something has changed.*)

> (*And the two are squeezed.*)

> (*And the moment is not romantic or hot or sexy.*)

Honey –

LURIE. Am I – ?

JUNE. Yeah.

LURIE. – pinching you?

JUNE. Just a little yeah –

LURIE. Sorry. So sorry.

> (**LURIE** *tries to make things better. But he can't.*)

I'll, I will –

JUNE. Oh for goodness sake, Lurie.

LURIE. I know. I um.

JUNE. *Lurie.*

>   (**LURIE** *stretches himself out in the tub beside* **JUNE.***)*

LURIE. Oh there, see? There: there it is.

>   *(But it doesn't look it, and* **JUNE** *is squished.)*

JUNE. It is huh?

>   (**LURIE** *shifts.)*

OW.

LURIE. Oh God.

JUNE. Just, just...

>   *(In one move* **LURIE** *is out of the tub and sitting back on the closed toilet seat. He grins at* **JUNE.***)*

Really Lurie? I just wanted you to sit quietly with me.

>   (**JUNE** *lies back in the tub.)*

I just wanted you, and me, to enjoy the morning and this room and this tub.

LURIE. Aren't you even hungry a little?

>   (**LURIE** *begins to fiddle with the tile at his feet.)*

JUNE. Because this tub is just *wonderful.* Don't you think?

I say: we do this room next. That's how much I love it.

That is how wonderful I think this tub is –

Which we will *have* to keep; which I am so glad we moved.

It looks marvelous over here. Don't you agree? Don't you think?

LURIE. Not very clean.

JUNE. You weren't worried about dirty ten minutes ago. Ten minutes ago you were rolling all around this tub naked.

LURIE. Dusty.

JUNE. So don't start about dirt now.

LURIE. Years and years ground up and spread all over the floor, into the air.

JUNE. Shh and just listen to our house with me.

LURIE. And not just dusty. It's cold, too. This whole room is very: cold.

JUNE. It's the tile.

LURIE. Outside it's pushing ninety. Outside it's like an oven. But in here –

JUNE. It's the porcelain. Listen with me.

LURIE. – freezing.

JUNE. Honey, *listen.* You can hear this whole house breathing.

(Both sit.)

(Both listen.)

Through the walls and then down from the ceilings and up through the floors.

LURIE. Through the tile?

JUNE. *Yes.*

LURIE. It's pretty thick tile.

>   *(A piece of tile breaks off in his hand.)*

>   *(But **JUNE**'s eyes are closed as she listens.)*

Maybe not so thick.

>   *(**LURIE** picks at the floor.)*

>   *(Once resilient sealant crumbles under his fingers.)*

Crumble.

JUNE. Shh.

>   *(**LURIE** plays with a loose tile.)*

LURIE. Crumble, crumble, crumble...

JUNE. After all those years of people, of families, rushing *up*stairs and *down*stairs.

And birthdays and Christmas' and babies –

LURIE. Dust, dust, dust...

JUNE. This house finally gets to breathe.

>   *(The house creaks softly.)*

With us.

>   *(The house creaks loudly.)*

LURIE. Asthma.

>   *(**LURIE** coughs.)*

>   *(More tiles crumble and dust rises into the air.)*

>   *(**JUNE** turns to **LURIE** sharply and takes in the debris.)*

JUNE. What are you doing?

LURIE. It broke. It's broken. See?

JUNE. Stop.

LURIE. Look.

JUNE. We'll fix it.

LURIE. We shouldn't have moved that tub. Now the floor's all in pieces, see? We ruined it.

JUNE. Not "we." Who's the one who didn't want to have someone in to do it for us?

LURIE. We can't call out for every little –

JUNE. Having our bathroom floor break apart into pieces –

LURIE. Paying someone to renovate the way your friends do costs too –

JUNE. The Realtor, and the Inspector, too, said this tub was originally over here anyway, so we. *Restored it.* We are *restoring.* I am not – . You – . My friends have nothing to do with this, just leave it.

LURIE. We should just take it easy: little by little: it's not all going to look perfect all at once.

JUNE. Well now it looks broken all at once.

> (**JUNE** *looks at* **LURIE.**)

> (**LURIE** *looks at* **JUNE.**)

But yes, okay, yes. Little by little.

LURIE. I'll. I'll patch that all up.

> (**LURIE** *nods to the crushed and crumbled floor.*)

JUNE. Sure.

LURIE. Okay.

JUNE. Sure.

LURIE. I *will.*

JUNE. Well with the curtains in here we won't even notice.

LURIE. Look at us. We're adults. Sewing curtains, ruining floors.

JUNE. Oh.

Oh, no, no, no.

(**LURIE** *looks at* **JUNE.**)

(**JUNE** *points to different parts of herself.*)

JUNE. What part of me says Pinterest to you, Lurie?

LURIE. Babe –

JUNE. Oh no, no, no.

LURIE. Babe –

JUNE. On sale. So it's *fine.*

LURIE. We can't.

JUNE. Sage. Beautiful color.

LURIE. We can't afford.

JUNE. Next check: new towels.

LURIE. The old are fine.

JUNE. The old are thin.

LURIE. But the old are *ours.*

JUNE. Oh Lurie.

LURIE. They work perfectly well.

JUNE. Oh Lurie.

LURIE. After showers. On all the bits.

JUNE. We can't start our new life with thin flimsy towels, Lurie.

LURIE. We have two other bathrooms. We don't even need this bathroom.

JUNE. We can't start our new life with thin flimsy towels. What would people think when they came to visit if we had thin flimsy towels hanging in this bathroom?

LURIE. Would they care? I don't even think they'd even –

JUNE. They would think, when they saw those thin flimsy towels, that we are thin flimsy people with thin flimsy lives.

LURIE. But the water's not even running in here yet. We don't need *new* curtains and *new* towels to show off, if we're not going to use this bathroom because the water's not even –

JUNE. Oh see now: that's why the plumber's coming.

LURIE. Plumber.

JUNE. Yes.

LURIE. Why?

JUNE. Monday.

LURIE. June.

JUNE. He's going to redo all the wiring.

LURIE. You seriously just called it wiring.

JUNE. Well that is why he is doing it because we are not *plumbers*.

Lurie.

LURIE. Plumbers charge.

JUNE. So glad he could do evenings. I almost died and went straight to heaven when I found that out. I was going to offer to pay extra –

LURIE. *Extra?* June, we cannot fix it all right away. It's going to take time –

JUNE. I don't want to hear about time and waiting, Lurie. I think: I think we've waited enough.

LURIE. ...

...

I know.

JUNE. Wait to finish school.

LURIE. I know, I know.

JUNE. Wait to find a job.

LURIE. June.

JUNE. Wait to find the *right* kind of job.

LURIE. We wanted everything to be –

JUNE. Wait to start trying –

LURIE. Come here.

> (**JUNE** *doesn't.*)

JUNE. Whoever we fill this house with will be perfect. But we've waited enough.

If we wait anymore, this house won't get done at all ever. I'm seeing every little thing gets attended to, to help make our family happen. Every little thing –

LURIE. *Costs.* It all *costs.*

JUNE. You don't love this house?

LURIE. I... I do.

JUNE. Well you're not acting like it. You are acting like we didn't work –

LURIE. We did –

JUNE. Like we didn't save –

LURIE. We did –

JUNE. Like every weekend we didn't hunt for a house to make a home. For so long.

And none of them were right. None of them were perfect. Until this one. We saw this one, and we fell in love because it's right, because it's perfect. And we agreed.

LURIE. Agreed *is*. Agreed gets tricky, now –

JUNE. To go without trips. And we agreed –

LURIE. Agreed loops around and kind of –

JUNE. To go without dinners out and all those little things, that can just eat up our extra money –

LURIE. It's not.

See it's not really *extra* and that, that, that's exactly my point exactly. We can't keep spending money we don't actually have.

JUNE. And you joked how we would even eat nothing but bread and margarine for supper.

LURIE. Ha.

JUNE. Bread and margarine for supper for *years* even, you said, *you said,* if that's what it would take for us to make this house our own.

LURIE. Margarine's not even a thing anymore June. And, and, and *margarine,* on a thirty year fixed rate? That is. That is. It *is* a joke. Bread and *margarine*?

JUNE. It could be cheez-wiz. You know what I mean.

LURIE. It's ridiculous.

(**JUNE** *looks at* **LURIE.**)

(**JUNE** *might be about to pounce.*)

(But she doesn't.)

(She eases.)

JUNE. Well, we have to do at least a little bit of work right away because there's the dinner party.

> **(LURIE** *looks at* **JUNE.)**

> **(LURIE** *might be about to pounce.)*

> *(But he eases as well.)*

> *(As* **JUNE** *speaks from inside the tub with her eyes closed* **LURIE** *takes in the space.)*

This place can't look like a wreck with these neighbor people coming over here.

We need to make a good impression. We need to make the *best* impression.

Especially considering this house needs so much work. We need to accent its positives.

And you know what, you know what: I don't understand exactly why you are being so difficult, Lurie, honestly. We can't stop now. We have to keep working. We have to make this house our home. I'm right, you know I'm right.

> **(LURIE** *jiggles a piece of tile in the middle of the floor.)*

Stop *messing* with that floor, Lurie. It's bad enough as it is.

> **(JUNE** *leans her head back on the rim of the tub.)*

> *(She closes her eyes.)*

> *(Quiet.)*

(**LURIE** *holds up a square of tile, examines it.*)

LURIE. This room is like every decade of the last hundred years all smashed together in one –

JUNE. Just pop it back.

LURIE. Dragging this tub across the floor was a very bad idea.

(*More tile comes loose in his hand.*)

JUNE. Oh. See. There, now look. I'm calling the contractor.

LURIE. Don't, don't, don't do that, now. I can fix it. I'll fix it. See?

(*As he tries to fit the tile into the floor, another tile comes loose.*)

JUNE. "See." See? He asks me. I see. I see fine because I see what you did. Look what you did, Lurie, honestly, I –

LURIE. I'll get some / glue.

JUNE. Glue? No, uh-uh. Just leave it. Just...don't touch anymore.

LURIE. I just wanna –

JUNE. Lawrence Walker if you don't *quit* touching all over that floor. I said don't.

Just don't. Just leave it alone.

(**JUNE** *leans back in the tub and closes her eyes.*)

(**LURIE** *sits.*)

(*Then.*)

(**LURIE** *can't help it.*)

(**LURIE** *goes back to fiddling with the floor.*)

JUNE. The more you poke at it the more it'll need to get fixed.

(The house seems to sigh.)

And I *will* call the contractor.

LURIE. Don't call the contractor.

(The house seems to sigh.)

JUNE. Watch me.

LURIE. If you're going to call anybody, call LeRoy.

JUNE. Your brother can't do the whole house, Lurie. We have been over this. He's got his own family. We can't keep asking him to come all the way out here on his days off to fix our house.

*(Sunlight streams in through the window, preternaturally illuminating **LURIE** and airborne particles of dust and plaster.)*

(More coughing.)

(This time it is louder than before.)

Why are you standing there like that?

Why are you just standing in the sun like that not moving, just staring?

What is the matter with you, Lurie?

LURIE. Sh.

Listen.

(They do.)

Coughing.

(But there is nothing now.)

JUNE. I don't hear anything.

LURIE. *Listen.*

> *(A short cough, very faint.)*

> **(LURIE** *is still rubbing his fingers together.)*

> **(LURIE** *stares at the patch of floor.)*

LURIE. See?

 That.

JUNE. This is an old house.

> **(LURIE** *gets close to the patch of floor.)*

LURIE. And hair.

JUNE. Hair?

LURIE. I felt –

JUNE. Hair.

LURIE. Under...the tile.

JUNE. You did not.

LURIE. Naw: yeah. Yeah I did.

JUNE. How under the tile did you feel hair?

LURIE. Hair.

> **(LURIE** *kneels down on the floor and begins to carefully remove squares of tile, which come loose easily.)*

> **(JUNE** *leans back against the tub.)*

JUNE. For crying out loud.

> *(The tinny sound of a music box can be heard.)*

(The light from the window shines brightly.)

(Puffs of dust curl up from the floor as **LURIE** *works.)*

(We hear coughing, this time more human than before and then finally a very deep intake of breath, as if someone is gasping for fresh air.)

(At this, **LURIE** *backs up and away again, colliding with the tub.)*

JUNE. What is it now, Lurie? More hair?

*(**JUNE** laughs.)*

*(**LURIE** gulps.)*

LURIE. J...j...just look.

JUNE. If we hadn't been married six years I'd think you deserved to be locked up.

(She pulls herself up and over the rim of the tub and kisses him on the back of the head.)

My own little Loony Tune –

*(**JUNE** stops suddenly as views the now large patch of untiled floor.)*

(Long pause.)

LURIE. How long...do you think it's been under there?

JUNE. I don't know.

LURIE. ' couple of years?

JUNE. I *said* I don't *know.*

LURIE. There's no smell and the skin still looks –

JUNE. Alive.

LURIE. I *knew* I felt hair. I told you, see? I told you I felt hair. It's. It's a lot of hair. White people's hair.

JUNE. Sh.

LURIE. Well –

JUNE. Just –

LURIE. Still soft. Not brittle. Which you'd think –

JUNE. Sh. Sh. Sh.

LURIE. We should call –

> (**JUNE** *begins shaking her head back and forth.*)

Hospital? Police? Probably way too late for hospital.

So.

Police. Or the station. I could call the police *and* the station. Can you believe this shit?

Bill Blake lives for this shit. He'd be right here in our front yard. We make fun of this stuff: like how can you not *know* and then here we *are*. Here this *is*. I could be captioning the news from my our house, June. The stories I bring to the world are happening in my own –. In my own –. This is, this is *wild*.

Police, then Bill.

JUNE. Cement.

LURIE. Uhhh what?

JUNE. Something airtight that will seal it all up. It should be waterproof, too. This is a bathroom. There's a lot of moisture and I don't want that smelling up our whole house.

LURIE. No.

N,n,n,n,no.

JUNE. Why not?

LURIE. Uh.

Because it's a person and not, not, not some *thing* to be pushed down somewhere and forgotten. Are you out of your mind?

JUNE. Don't talk to me like that. No. Of course not –

LURIE. Well what are you talking about cement for?

JUNE. This is our house.

LURIE. Which is why we're going to call somebody to take whatever, whoever, this is, away.

JUNE. No.

LURIE. *What?*

JUNE. We will mix some cement and cover it all up.

LURIE. *June.*

JUNE. All I saw was hair, really, there's nothing wrong with using cement to cover up hair, is there?

LURIE. You didn't just see hair.

JUNE. I did.

LURIE. Does that look like just hair to you?

JUNE. Yes.

LURIE. Look.

JUNE. No.

LURIE. Look for real.

JUNE. I don't need to.

LURIE. There's forehead, June. Pale, almost gray. *Look.*

JUNE. *You* look.

LURIE. Dead hair and dead skin. We're calling somebody.

JUNE. I said cement, Lurie, don't make me say it again.

LURIE. Please listen to me for once.

JUNE. Please, please listen to *me*.

Just, just, just think.

Think about it for a little bit.

If we call someone about this.

This house. Our house.

Is going to fill with people.

A whole lot of people.

Trampling in and out and all around in our house.

Bill. Bill will trample in and out and all around our house.

You can't even stand him at holiday parties.

So, so, so, TV people and YouTube people and podcast people and, and, and adoption agencies

They want

They want

They want to find perfect homes.

Perfect homes do not pop up in Google searches with dead hair foreheads in the hashtag line.

Everything will have to stop.

If we call someone.

LURIE. I find dead white people's hair under my bathroom floor, I think everything *should* stop.

JUNE. That is respectability politics, right there. It shouldn't have to. It should not need to.

LURIE. What are you... What is happening right now?

JUNE. You promised about this house. We agree –

LURIE. This is different.

JUNE. We need this house to be perfect –

LURIE. June –

JUNE. – for the new neighbors. For the adoption lady –

LURIE. The adoption lady.

JUNE. Yes.

Yes, yes, yes.

Please, please, Lurie.

Let's just forget about hair and coughing, and, and, and –

LURIE. Foreheads.

JUNE. Yes.

LURIE. Dead foreheads.

JUNE. NO.

LURIE. How can we live in here wi, wi, with that?

JUNE. I told you: Cement.

LURIE. There's something *dead* in our *floor.*

JUNE. Let's eat. Let's get lunch. Pot roast. We'll go buy some. And the paper –

LURIE. Please, June –

JUNE. – and, and, and we'll cook, and we'll eat.

And we'll cement.

LURIE. Uhhhhh...

JUNE. And then we will read the paper and we will forget all about dead hair and dead foreheads. And we will wait for our towels and have the plumber come and –

LURIE. What if somebody asks about it?

JUNE. Who? Who would ask about?

LURIE. Anybody. Somebody. If they –

JUNE. They won't.

LURIE. What if somebody comes looking for it?

JUNE. They won't.

LURIE. We don't know that. How do we know that?

JUNE. Let me have this one thing.

LURIE. This is not the same as a labradoodle, June.

JUNE. All I want is this one thing.

LURIE. This is very different. Very, very different –

JUNE. We've tried everything, everything else.

LURIE. This is, this is –

JUNE. Doctors and kale diets and shots and procedures and, and, and

Nothing

Nothing

Nothing

Worked.

LURIE. I know that.

I know that, I –

JUNE. This house and that adoption lady are the only way, Lurie.

LURIE. Someone will find out. This all feels wrong.

JUNE. This house is the only way to have a family.

     (**LURIE** *looks at* **JUNE.***)*

JUNE. I'm right.

...

Aren't I right?

...

Lurie?

...

Lurie.

...

Lurie?

...

Please answer.

...

(**LURIE** *looks at* **JUNE.**)

JUNE. You do want a family, too, Lurie, don't you? This is for us. Our home. I need you. Here. Beside me.

(**LURIE** *looks at* **JUNE.**)

(**JUNE** *smiles at* **LURIE.**)

So please. Answer.

LURIE. This house.

And that adoption lady.

Are the only way.

JUNE. Exactly. Yes. So it's got to be cement. We've worked too hard to have someone else's problem ruin everything for us. Because this is not our problem. We did not do anything wrong, did we?

LURIE. I guess not.

JUNE. No. Absolutely not. Did we hurt anybody and try to cover it all up with tile, with a tub?

LURIE. Not yet –

JUNE. We are not bad people.

LURIE. – but we're about to.

JUNE. We did not hurt anybody and leave it for someone else to clean up.

And I do not clean up other people's messes. I am not the maid.

My mother spent thirty years, thirty grime filled, piss filled –

LURIE. This is not the same.

JUNE. I won't do that in my own house.

LURIE. No one is asking you to –

JUNE. Should we lose *out*, just because we moved *in*?

LURIE. Baby –

JUNE. We are just trying to get everyone else gets.

LURIE. Baby –

JUNE. No, no we should *not* lose out, Lurie, we should not.

>(**LURIE** *looks at* **JUNE**.)

>(**JUNE** *looks at* **LURIE**.)

>(**LURIE** *looks at* **JUNE**.)

>(**JUNE** *looks at* **LURIE**.)

Cement.

It's the only way.

(The house creaks as the lights go down on **JUNE** *and* **LURIE**.*)*

(Later that night...)

(Light slowly seeps in through a window on another part of the stage.)

(The kitchen.)

(It is a bit more updated than the bathroom. A table and chairs. Perhaps one or two leftover moving boxes as yet unpacked.)

(Moonlight streams through the kitchen window.)

(The sound of a metal spoon against glass. The sound of lips smacking together. After a few moments, both sounds stop.)

(A hand reaches up from under the table and places an empty jam jar with a metal spoon in it on the tableclothed table top as the darkness returns.)

(The house seems to moan.)

(When light returns **JUNE** *and* **LURIE** *are at the table.)*

*(***LURIE** *reads the paper.)*

*(***JUNE** *sits making a list.)*

JUNE. Towels,

Curtains,

Carpet,

Doorknobs –

(Creaaaaak.)

(Both are startled.)

It's. Just the house settling. It's so old.

(The house rattles.)

(A faint deep breathing can be heard.)

(In and out.)

(In and out.)

(Like the wind.)

(But not quite.)

LURIE. Settling.

JUNE. This house, yes, it's old.

LURIE. Huh.

*(**LURIE** returns to his paper.)*

*(**JUNE** returns, silently this time, to her work.)*

*(**LURIE** looks over the corner of his paper at the house.)*

*(Next, he looks over the corner of his paper at **JUNE**.)*

(Darkness.)

(Creeeaak.)

(The creaking gives way to the very faint sound of water running through pipes.)

(Lights come upon **LURIE** *and* **JUNE** *at the kitchen table a sandwich sits before each of them.)*

*(***LURIE*** *looks down at his plate.)*

(Before reaching for her sandwich **JUNE** *stops, looks at* **LURIE**.)*

JUNE. Aren't you hungry?

LURIE. Bread and margarine was a joke.

JUNE. But you're always hungry.

LURIE. Bread and margarine was a joke, I thought.

JUNE. It's not margarine, it's a spread. I'm thinking new shutters, so get used to it.

LURIE. At least, it was *supposed* to be a joke.

JUNE. Eat.

LURIE. We never bought that pot roast.

JUNE. The housewarming's next week, we'll have it then. For now, you'll only make it worse if you think about it: just eat it.

LURIE. So no meat.

JUNE. Next week. But I made jam for dessert.

*(***LURIE*** *pokes his sandwich.)*

LURIE. There isn't enough grocery money for maybe some pie? A little crust for some pie? A cookie or two?

JUNE. The front hall needs paint, so no.

LURIE. One can of paint equals dessert?

JUNE. One can of paint equals please just eat.

LURIE. What about pasta? That's cheap. Or rice. Or couscous.

JUNE. This is more romantic. We can tell our children about how you joked we'd eat bread and margarine –

LURIE. Joked, yeah.

JUNE. Bread and margarine for *years*, even, if that's what it took to make a home for them.

LURIE. Do they care about paint though?

JUNE. And we'll all laugh about it when they're all grown and we're sitting out there on that porch and they're visiting here from homes of their own.

LURIE. Well. No one's laughing now. Bread and margarine is not very funny at all when it's sitting in front of you begging to get eaten. It's. Well. Actually a little pathetic.

'You ask me.

JUNE. Don't get sulky.

LURIE. I am a little sulky.

JUNE. You are a little sulky.

Let me cheer you up.

(**LURIE** *looks up at* **JUNE.**)

Let me cheer you up.

LURIE. I dunno. I might be *too* sulky. The hunger and all.

(**JUNE** *rises.*)

(*She holds out her hand.*)

JUNE. Come on.

(**LURIE** *looks up.*)

LURIE. I dunno. It might be a waltz or something.

(**JUNE** *finds the right music on her watch.*)

JUNE. Okay. No "waltz or something."

(Tango music* plays.)

*(**LURIE** cocks his head, considering.)*

JUNE. I got this. Come on.

*(**LURIE** stands.)*

*(**JUNE** and **LURIE** begin to dance.)*

*(As they do, it is obvious that **JUNE** is distracted by various parts of the kitchen.)*

LURIE. What's the matter?

JUNE. New doorknobs. I was right.

LURIE. I thought you were cheering me up.

JUNE. I am.

(They dance again.)

(But then.)

*(**JUNE**'s attention shifts to the kitchen and its failings.)*

*(**LURIE** works to keep up the dance and his moves become edgy.)*

*(Their dancing sharpens until **JUNE** breaks away.)*

There's just so much to do. Backsplashes. What do you think?

---

* A license to produce *Feeding Beatrice* does not include a performance license for any third-party or copyrighted music. Licensees should create an original composition or use music in the public domain. For further information, please see the Music and Third Party Materials Use Note on page iii.

Honestly, I've got lists coming out of my ears. I've got to keep at this or nothing will get finished. I'm sorry, babe. When this house is finished I'll make it up to you.

LURIE. Backsplashes?

JUNE. We'll dance all over the place. We'll re-christen every room.

LURIE. We can't afford –

JUNE. But for now –

> (**JUNE** *sits, attends to her list, eats her sandwich.*)

LURIE. Backsplashes.

> (*Darkness.*)

> (*The sound of water running through pipes.*)

> (*Light.*)

> (**JUNE** *and* **LURIE** *at the kitchen table.*)

> (**JUNE** *is working on her list.*)

> (**LURIE** *reads a paper.*)

> (**LURIE** *cocks his head, turns down a corner of the paper.*)

Are you running a bath?

JUNE. A bath?

LURIE. It sounds like there's water running.

JUNE. No. It's the house like I've said.

It's old. It makes noises.

LURIE. We shouldn't use that tub.

JUNE. Am I using the tub?

LURIE. It might break the floor.

JUNE. No-one-is-using-the-tub, Lurie. The water is cut off from that room anyway, remember?

LURIE. And that floor is, that floor is.

JUNE. Fixed. I fixed it. I took that grout pump and sealed it all up and pressed that cement over that and. And your brother is coming tomorrow to do the plumbing, to help with the plumbing, and.

LURIE. What if –

JUNE. I fixed the floor. LeRoy will fix the pipes. You don't need to think about that bathroom any more. It's all taken care of.

> (**LURIE** *looks at* **JUNE.**)

> (**JUNE** *goes back to her work.*)

> (**LURIE** *goes back behind the newspaper corner.*)

> (**JUNE** *presses her watch and music plays*.*)

> (*Darkness.*)

> (*Lights come up on the bathroom.*)

> (**LEROY** *stands in the middle of the room.*)

> (*He looks the room over.*)

> (*Some pipe is exposed and he looks at that, but he eventually looks at the hella botched up floor.*)

---

* A license to produce *Feeding Beatrice* does not include a performance license for any third-party or copyrighted music. Licensees should create an original composition or use music in the public domain. For further information, please see the Music and Third Party Materials Use Note on page iii.

(**LEROY** *kneels and rubs his hand over the tile.*)

(*No traces of dust, loose tile, or dead anything can be seen.*)

(*Creeeaaak.*)

(**LURIE** *enters.*)

LURIE. The...tile was breaking –

LEROY. So you tried to fix it.

LURIE. I *did* fix it.

LEROY. Then how come this floor looks like the inside of a fluffer-nutter sandwich? Cement? Everything's all slathered like the peanut butter and the marshmallow fluff are having their way with each other.

LURIE. That's, that's an image right there. And it was June who did all that.

LEROY. What business do you all have tiling floor?

LURIE. D-I-Y, little brother of mine, D-I-Y. Besides, you're here to fix the pipes, not the tile. Stay in your lane. Come...come over here.

LEROY. My man got a bathroom so big he can say in it "Come over here." Can you believe that? Can you *believe* that?

LURIE. We moved the tub so. So we need the plumbing hooked up over.

(**LEROY** *touches the floor.*)

LeRoy, stop messing with that floor.

LEROY. Alright, alright, alright. Pipe down now.

(**LEROY** *chuckles.*)

LURIE. Clever.

LEROY. I think so, yeah.

LURIE. June wants this room ready for the housewarming.

LEROY. Housewarming.

LURIE. Uh yeah.

LEROY. Sure is quiet around here.

LURIE. Just –

LEROY. When I drove up I swear I could hear the sweat sliding down my back. You need air conditioning in here, man. We absorb heat, or d'you forget living way out here?

LURIE. Air conditioning. You know how much it'd cost to air condition this whole house? Shoot, just this bathroom alone.

LEROY. You can do anything you want on the insides of these old houses.

It's the outside you gotta cut the red tape about.

LURIE. The little old couple that lived here before us? The only real change they made the whole time they were here was to move that tub.

LEROY. Naw, man, naw. You got to open your eyes. There's a hundred years easy in this bathroom alone.

LURIE. It's all too much to do in a week.

June's got gold dust in her eyes.

LEROY. You even meet any of these neighbors yet?

LURIE. ...It's summer.

LEROY. Yeah, uh-huh...

LURIE. Vacations: you know.

(**LEROY** *gives* **LURIE** *a look.*)

What? People do. They go away. On vacations.

LEROY. I mean, it's quiet, sure, but c'mon, Lawrence, man.

LURIE. What?

LEROY. The place isn't *deserted*. I saw a couple in little jogging shorts running along that wide street.

LURIE. Uh-huh.

LEROY. And I saw one of those nanny women pushing a carriage.

Twin babies splayed out sleepy in their seats.

Woman was sturdy, thick: Island.

LURIE. You can't say things like –

LEROY. I mean her presence. Everything was rated G. I waved.

LURIE. Of course you did.

LEROY. She was over on, over on –

LURIE. Briar Cliff.

LEROY. So you know her.

LURIE. Nope. Don't know her.

LEROY. I'm putting a pin in that: You knew exactly who I meant. Because there are three black people out here, so you knew exactly who I meant.

LURIE. ...Briar Cliff. Yeah. We've. Noticed. The stroller. Two babies. At once.

How can that be? How lucky. All at once. Of course I noticed: that stroller.

    (Creak.)

LEROY. ...These street names, man. "Carriage Hill," "Wisteria Lane," "Morningside."

' make you think you're someplace far away and special. In the city, they ' named so you know exactly where you are. Roosevelt, Washington. A Martin Luther King Boulevard tells you exactly where the Dr. Reverend was intended to be, and where you are intended to stay.

LURIE. Don't start.

LEROY. Show me one MLK street out here.

LURIE. Do not start.

LEROY. And I will lick all that cement up out your floor.

LURIE. Well, yeah, it's cement, so have fun.

LEROY. Plenty nice houses near us, near Ma.

LURIE. Okay, okay, see.

LEROY. Okay yes, now. Now I admit. I am starting something.

LURIE. Can you maybe just even *look* at the pipes?

LEROY. You meet the neighbors yet?

LURIE. You need something cool to drink? While you're working? I'll get you something. What do you want?

LEROY. Plenty of houses by Ma. Old Mrs. Greeson's house is for sale. Big. Roomy.

Plenty of room for babies. Plenty of room for a whole mess of sons. That's what you should ask for. Sons.

LURIE. Just healthy.

LEROY. A house full of boys is exactly what June needs to snap her out of this funk.

LURIE. It's not. It not a funk.

LEROY. She hasn't been the same since she lost that baby. I know it. You know it. Ma's tried to talk to her.

LURIE. ...You're right. You all've been great.

LEROY. Boys. House full.

LURIE. Sure... You want something cool? To, to... June is fine. She is okay.

LEROY. Why she drag you all the way out here, grabbing for things just that far out of touch, if she's okay? That house near us was cute, real cute.

LURIE. She's. Always been very. Driven. Determined. She wants a family. We both do want a family. She wants a home of her own. Different from the way she grew up.

She's wanted that since we met. Nothing's changed. She's always said.

And she's always been: Determined. She has the strength to go after what she wants. Not everyone can do that. June's unique that way. Her plans are an extension of that. Perfectly natural.

LEROY. You gonna find out what's *very* natural when you meet these neighbors.

LURIE. *LeRoy.*

LEROY. Because you can buy a house out here, you can have your kids out here and play frontier-man with them. You can invite these new neighbors over for breakfast, lunch, and dinner – hors d'oeuvres, even – but that isn't gonna change a thing about the way these people see you. You remember that when it comes to your housewarming.

LURIE. It is just a dinner party, LeRoy. We're not integrating a Little Rock school, we're starting a family.

LEROY. It is always Little Rock. This is still the United States, isn't it? Twenty-four-seven: abuse served a la carte.

LURIE. Here we go.

LEROY. Abuse of the soul, of the heart, of the mind. Any kind of people these new neighbors of yours come into contact with, they gonna abuse. Why?

LURIE. Why.

LEROY. Because these people *are* America. They are abuse *in-car-nate*. How else they get so rich? How else they get so much all for themselves?

LURIE. A lot of them work for what they have. *We* work for what we have.

LEROY. Yeah, they working. They working for them*selves*. For every dollar they make, ten, fifteen cents could go to someone really need help.

LURIE. How do you know they don't do that? How do you know they don't give –

LEROY. None of these people's pockets got holes, that's what I'm saying. How else these houses get to look like this?

LURIE. The pipes.

LEROY. Abuse. In-carn –

LURIE. LeRoy.

LEROY. You cannot expect, you cannot expect, to come waltzing in here, into their neighborhood –

LURIE. Our. Our neighborhood. We own this house, now.

LEROY. You cannot expect to come waltzing into America's way-back-yard, and have them act friendly, play all nice, while you two play Barbie Dream House.

LURIE. Regular plumbers don't talk this much.

LEROY. You cannot expect that at all, and I'll tell you why. They gonna look you up, they gonna look you down, and then they gonna eat you up. So my question is. My question is.

Why? My big brother – I mean you ' supposed to be my older and wiser brother.

LURIE. I am, I am that. The genes dried up after me. Case in point. This conversation.

LEROY. My question is: Why do you want to invite America to dinner? Why do you want America to ring your front door? You inviting America to dinner but America does not eat food. America never ate food. Souls. America gets hungry for souls. Keep that simmering in your mind when you greet those new neighbors and maybe you'll be okay.

> (**LURIE** *looks at* **LEROY.**)

I'm right, Lawrence, I am right.

> (**LEROY** *grins.*)

> (**LURIE** *shakes his head.*)

LURIE. No.

LEROY. Also.

LURIE. No.

LEROY. Also remember: all this acting proper business, that these new neighbors do takes *energy*. Year after year, day after day, minute by minute by second. It takes so much that by now they ain't even half interested in food. Go to any fancy restaurant. Go to any fancy restaurant and look at the plate. Hardly any food on it. Souls. Souls is what they all into, Lurie, not real food at all, that's why they don't care they're only buying little bits of it at a time. The spit behind their lips, on their tongues, just can't wait to coat itself all over some rich delicious souls. All those years of living this way's dried up their own souls.

They need more. These people get together for a party the last thing they want is a clean house and chip and dip. If you and June throw a party, better be ready for these people to sniff around for fresh soouuul.

LURIE. Cut that out.

LEROY. They gonna look around, they gonna hope beyond hope, that some deep dark part of your soul mingles with some deep, deep part of their soul, if only for a little bit, if only so they can tell their friends after. And if they can't get that. Well then. Why bother with you at all?

LURIE. We have met *no one*, let me remind you.

LEROY. We are the bread of life to them, Lurie. To consume, to set aside, as they wish.

LURIE. Well when we meet them, then we can find out –

LEROY. I don't need to meet them.

LURIE. June and I will meet them. We'll tell you all about them.

LEROY. So far. How many times these people had to tell you to turn your music down?

LURIE. Um, *none*.

LEROY. How many times these people smelled collard greens from June's kitchen?

LURIE. We eat lighter these days.

LEROY. Ham hocks?

LURIE. LeRoy –

LEROY. How many of these people have you taught to bump?

LURIE. Aww, man.

LEROY. Grind.

LURIE. Absolutely none.

LEROY. Right. You ain't offering up your soul.

LURIE. Just. Fix. The pipes.

LEROY. When did the smell of ganga –

LURIE. Ganga?

LEROY. Reefer.

LURIE. *Reefer?*

LEROY. Mari-ja-wan-a, forties, afro-shhheeen. When did all them smells reach the Joneses?

LURIE. I don't have to tell you not every black person smokes refer, drinks forties, uses –

LEROY. I know that and you know that but not all of these neighbors know that. You're not feeding them in the manner to which they have become accustomed, my brutha. You're starving them. They're so hungry for you, they think they can taste you already, but they're still not gonna come knocking 'cause you all don't got what they need to be satisfied.

And *that's* why no neighbors, none of *these* neighbors, are gonna come over here to visit you and June.

LURIE. Me and June are fine.

LEROY. Bet me five dollars no one's going to come knocking on that door.

LURIE. You need five dollars?

LEROY. I want to bet, I want to bet, I want to bet.

LURIE. You need five dollars.

LEROY. A hundred.

LURIE. I'm not taking your money.

LEROY. You know you're gonna lose.

LURIE. It's summer. These people go places.

LEROY. Lose, lose, lose. You know what. Just pay me now.

LURIE. One hundred dollars?

LEROY. You and June think you can live here without offering yourselves up. You think you can live here and just mind your own business. No, no, and nope.

Pay me.

Pay me.

Pay me.

LURIE. I don't care if they come.

LEROY. June does. June surely does. That is why I am here. So, so you do. Summer, winter, spring, or fall. Rain or shine or snow. Ain't no one gonna step up to that front door and ring that bell.

> (*A doorbell rings.*)

> (**LURIE** *and* **LEROY** *look at each other.*)

> (**LURIE** *smiles at* **LEROY**.)

> (**LURIE** *holds our his hand to* **LEROY**...)

> (*...and uncurls his fingers...*)

> (*Lights out on the bathroom.*)

> (*Lights up on* **JUNE** *and* **BEATRICE**.)

> (*The kitchen.*)

BEATRICE. Do you want to live here a long time or a short time?

JUNE. ...We just got here.

BEATRICE. So a long time.

JUNE. I hope.

> (*Pause.*)

> (**BEATRICE** *looks at* **JUNE**.)

(**JUNE** *looks at* **BEATRICE**, *but then is not sure where to look. It's confusing.*)

BEATRICE. Could I have some milk?

JUNE. Uhhh sure.

BEATRICE. Growing girls need lots of milk.

JUNE. Uhhh okay.

BEATRICE. It's just another way to help you get strong enough to leave your girl days behind.

(**JUNE** *pours milk.*)

(*And* **BEATRICE** *drinks it.*)

JUNE. Sure... You know...

BEATRICE. Beatrice.

JUNE. Beatrice. It is so nice to. To meet you: Our first guest.

BEATRICE. Oh yes, I know.

JUNE. You do?

BEATRICE. Mmm.

JUNE. Uh. Oh. Okay. Beatrice. Do you. Um. Live nearby?

BEATRICE. You like it here?

JUNE. We do.

BEATRICE. You don't ever want to move away?

JUNE. Not planning on it. Nope.

BEATRICE. Even though you're the only Negroes?

JUNE. Pardon?

BEATRICE. You're the only Negroes. On this street you're the only ones. I'm right. I'm not wrong.

JUNE. That's word's just. We don't use that word. Anymore.

BEATRICE. Oh. Oh, I'm sorry.

JUNE. Some people still don't know, I guess. Do...do your parents? Use that –

BEATRICE. But you *are* the only colored people –

JUNE. Or that one.

BEATRICE. Oh. Okay. I'm very sorry.

> (**BEATRICE** *looks down into her glass of milk.*)
>
> (*A very long pause.*)
>
> (**BEATRICE** *is very still.*)
>
> (**BEATRICE** *is so still that* **JUNE** *is not sure what to do.*)

JUNE. If. If your parents use those words, they shouldn't.

BEATRICE. *(To the glass of milk.)* They do. They very much do.

JUNE. It's okay.

BEATRICE. I'm sorry. I like Neeg. I *love* you. All of you. I want to run away with Frankie Lymon for keeps. "Teenager In Love" is the ultimate. And I just think. If I lived here a long time. Like you're planning. I'd get very lonely. Even if you're not lonely now. Because I'm here. Because I rang your bell. I might *get* lonely. Will you move then if you do?

JUNE. ...I don't know. I hope not. We like this house.

BEATRICE. Your kids might get lonely.

JUNE. We. Don't have kids. Not right now, anyway. Not yet.

BEATRICE. When you get some, if they don't like it here, then you'll move? Because they might be sad since they'd be the only Negroes.

JUNE. They'll have friends. And the word is black. Or it can be two words. African-American.

>   (**BEATRICE** *blinks.*)

>   (**BEATRICE** *smiles.*)

>   (**BEATRICE** *takes a drink of milk.*)

BEATRICE. But their friends won't be any of those things. Their friends will look like me.

And sometimes people just are not very nice. Sometimes people are very, very unkind.

They say ugly things. I know this. What will you do then?

JUNE. Well, my job would to be to –

BEATRICE. Can I have some more milk?

JUNE. ...Do you live on this street?

>   (**BEATRICE** *nods.*)

Up...up by the park?

>   (**BEATRICE** *shakes her head.*)

Down some?

>   (**BEATRICE** *nods her head.*)

Down some towards the end of the street?

>   (**BEATRICE** *shakes her head.*)

BEATRICE. But very close by.

JUNE. How close by?

BEATRICE. Can I have some of that milk?

>   (**JUNE** *pauses.*)

(But then gets the milk.)

BEATRICE. I'd do it. I'd be your kids' friend. I'd bring them cookies.

I make good ones. And you could pour us milk and we'll all eat – you can have some too. And we'll all eat and drink and none of us will be lonely. Won't that be the most fun?

That'd be the most fun. I can already tell.

JUNE. So we're neighbors.

BEATRICE. Mmm-mm.

JUNE. Your parents know where you are?

BEATRICE. It doesn't matter where I am. I'm grown.

JUNE. You just said you needed milk to get bigger.

*(**BEATRICE** cocks her head at **JUNE**.)*

BEATRICE. I like you.

JUNE. You should call them. So they don't worry.

BEATRICE.   They don't mind. My mother especially does not mind one bit. In the afternoon she just sits in her room. I can stay. As long as I want. I can do what you all do.

JUNE. You will be bored to tears.

BEATRICE. I can do what you all do all day.

*(**BEATRICE** looks at **JUNE**.)*

*(**BEATRICE** smiles at **JUNE**.)*

*(**JUNE** looks away.)*

JUNE. All we do is fix this house.

BEATRICE. I'll do that, and also the other things. I want to know about the other things.

When you're not in the house. What do you do when you're not in the house?

JUNE. Work, mostly.

BEATRICE. What's he do?

JUNE. Both of us.

BEATRICE. Oh. I understand. You have to work, too. He's in the cups?

       (**BEATRICE** *mimes taking a drink.*)

I have an uncle like that. His wife has to work, too.

       (**JUNE** *blinks.*)

JUNE. No, uh-uh. We both work because that's what people do. And we like it.

BEATRICE. My uncle's wife works in a shop. Do you work in a shop?

JUNE. A bank.

BEATRICE. *Really.* With all the money?

JUNE. ...

    ...

    ...

You have.

Some very.

Distinct ideas, um, um. I'd love to talk to your parents, about some of them –

BEATRICE. Well I would like to talk to that *bank* about you. My uncle's wife worked at that shop and the whole town nearly had a heart attack, her working with all those men around her like that. If you ask me that bank's all heroes letting you work there –

JUNE. They do not "let" me work there –

BEATRICE. What's Lurie do?

JUNE. He –

BEATRICE. Something *amazing* I'll bet.

JUNE. How do you know his name?

BEATRICE. Mmm?

JUNE. His name?

BEATRICE. I think this milk is warm? And I'd love something sweet. Do you have anything sweet?

> (**JUNE** *looks at* **BEATRICE.**)

> (**BEATRICE** *smiles at* **JUNE.**)

JUNE. ...He writes the news.

BEATRICE. Oooooooh.

JUNE. Captions. Captioning.

> (**JUNE** *wiggles her fingers as if typing.*)

> (**BEATRICE** *tilts her head to the side.*)

For TV.

...

For when people can't hear. For people who need to see it on a screen.

BEATRICE. TVeeee.

JUNE. Are you sure you don't want to borrow a phone to call?

BEATRICE. Channel four, five, or seven?

JUNE. Twenty-five.

BEATRICE. Twenty-*five*? How in the world do you expect me to believe *that*? There's no channel "twenty-*five*." How good can he be if he doesn't work for four, five, or seven?

JUNE. Well there are many channels –

BEATRICE. "Many channels." Ha. You're funny. I like funny people. A television set does not have many channels. You are very, very funny. I love that about your people. Just look at Sammy Davis, Jr.

JUNE. Beatrice –

BEATRICE. Or Johnny Mathis.

JUNE. What?

BEATRICE. You're right. Johnny Mathis not so much.

JUNE. Tell me your number. I'll call your parents.

BEATRICE. My father works for advertising. He loves Johnny Mathis very much.

JUNE. I'll bet.

BEATRICE. Are you a teller?

JUNE. What?

BEATRICE. At the bank.

JUNE. Oh. No, I am not.

BEATRICE. A secretary. Wow. Congratulations.

JUNE. I'm an officer.

(**BEATRICE** *blinks.*)

JUNE. I sign things. And I say yes and I say no. I'm in charge. Well. Half in charge. I have people who are also in charge of *me*.

BEATRICE. Of course.

JUNE. I could also walk you home. It's down the street you said?

BEATRICE. I'd love that milk.

JUNE. Yeah. Nope. You know, we're out of milk.

BEATRICE. Out? Out of milk?

JUNE. Fresh out.

>   (**BEATRICE** *looks at* **JUNE.**)
>
>   (**JUNE** *looks at* **BEATRICE.**)
>
>   (**BEATRICE** *half smiles at* **JUNE.**)
>
>   (*But* **JUNE** *does not budge.*)
>
>   (*Next,* **BEATRICE** *frowns.*)

BEATRICE. Please don't make me go home.

JUNE. It's kind of late.

BEATRICE. Please don't make me leave.

JUNE. I think it might be better.

BEATRICE. I like it here.

JUNE. You just got here.

BEATRICE. It's a...a quality I sense. Here.

JUNE. Uh-huh.

BEATRICE. You're good people in here. Very good. Very kind. I like it. It's different from where I. Please can I just have some milk please? I don't feel like going home. Okay? Please?

JUNE. ...

...

...Okay.

> (**JUNE** *goes to get more milk.*)
>
> (*Her watch goes off.*)
>
> (*It is the Tango music* from earlier.*)
>
> (*A ring tone.*)
>
> (**BEATRICE** *covers her ears and crouches.*)
>
> (**JUNE** *looks down at her watch and turns it off.*)
>
> (**JUNE** *notices* **BEATRICE.***)

Oh. It's just.

> (**JUNE** *holds up her wrist.*)
>
> (**BEATRICE** *eases a bit.*)

Old habits. I miss the music. I used to teach.

> (**BEATRICE** *regards the watch.*)

BEATRICE. I don't like school. I stopped going. My mother needed me at home so it's alright so I stopped going. I'm much better at cleaning anyway, she says.

JUNE. Not teaching-in-a-school-kind of teaching. Dance.

BEATRICE. Dance.

---

* A license to produce *Feeding Beatrice* does not include a performance license for any third-party or copyrighted music. Licensees should create an original composition or use music in the public domain. For further information, please see the Music and Third Party Materials Use Note on page iii.

JUNE. But we needed. Well. This –

*(***JUNE*** indicates the house.)*

So. Hello bank.

BEATRICE. Dance.

JUNE. Yes.

BEATRICE. *American Bandstand* kind of dancing or Lawrence Welk kind of dancing.

JUNE. Iiiiiii'd saaaaay: nada. Neither.

BEATRICE. I can't get enough of *American Bandstand.* I have to sneak, but I think Dick Clark is one of the dreamiest men alive, beside Senator Kennedy. Actually. *All those* Kennedys are very dreamy. My father says their bleeding hearts will soak this country red.

And they have too much money for their own good, but I adore them. And their teeth.

No one ever fixed my teeth but the Kennedys have wonderful teeth. To be Mrs. Kennedy for one day. Weeeeeee. Could you teach *me* to dance?

JUNE. Oh. Oh, I don't know.

BEATRICE. Please, please, please.

JUNE. I don't know.

BEATRICE. Oh please.

JUNE. What do you want to learn?

BEATRICE. That song in your hand. Let's dance to that.

JUNE. That's advanced. Advanced. Maybe the bunny-hop.

BEATRICE. No, no, no.

(She stops.)

You're. Are you playing a joke on me? Ha-ha. No. That song in your hand sounded tragic. And full of drama. And romance. I want that. I bet you were a good teacher. I bet it was horrible that day you gave it up.

JUNE. It was fine. I love this house.

BEATRICE. Teach me. Teach me: it will be the most fun, I promise, promise, promise.

JUNE. ...

...Okay.

BEATRICE. OKAY.

JUNE. Okay.

> (**JUNE** *gets into position.*)

> (**BEATRICE** *follows suit.*)

> (**JUNE** *turns on the music.*)

> (*They dance.*)

Tango.

BEATRICE. I'll say.

JUNE. It's all about power.

BEATRICE. *Power.*

JUNE. That's why I love it.

BEATRICE. Then I love it too.

JUNE. See, I ask you to dance –

BEATRICE. Because I'm the girl –

JUNE. Sure –

BEATRICE. On *American Bandstand* –

JUNE. I didn't know they show that anymore –

BEATRICE. On *American Bandstand* there's one boy and one girl. Everyone partners up.

No one's left alone. Or, if you're left alone, they don't film you, I think.

No one wants to see an *actual* lonely person on television. What's the point, right?

JUNE. See, I ask you to dance, you pretend it doesn't matter. You pretend you don't even care. Like this, see?

BEATRICE. Oooo.

JUNE. I ask. You don't care. I ask –

BEATRICE. I guess I don't care? But this isn't like *American Bandstand* at all –

JUNE. You dance when you decide it's time. You're in charge. Moment to moment.

Even when it looks like you aren't. Like this.

BEATRICE. I see.

JUNE. And when I'm ready –

BEATRICE. I'm still the girl.

JUNE. Yes.

BEATRICE. But. So. But what if I'm not ready to start.

JUNE. That doesn't matter.

BEATRICE. Well that's not fair.

JUNE. Well. No. Right. You're right. But then, well, then there's no dance.

BEATRICE. Well then good.

JUNE. Sure. But in order to dance. In this case. Dancing is good.

BEATRICE. Okay.

JUNE. I mean, if we want to *continue* dancing.

BEATRICE. I don't think I like this Tango.

JUNE. It's about push-pull. One person pushes, the other pulls. The two need each other.

BEATRICE. I don't. I don't need to be pushed and pulled.

JUNE. I guess not. Okay. Maybe the Tango –

BEATRICE. I like this though. Learning things.

JUNE. Pretty cool, huh?

BEATRICE. Sometimes I miss school. Other people.

JUNE. Homeschooling is like that, I heard. Is like that –

BEATRICE. If you were my mother, you could teach me everything you know. I'd listen to everything very carefully and follow every word. You'd be such a good mother. I can tell. It will be so fabulous when you have some children. I just know it.

> (**JUNE** *gets shy.*)

JUNE. Well. And now you know the Tango.

BEATRICE. All because of you. You're the most, June. I almost really do wish you were my mother.

> (**BEATRICE** *holds her hands up for a dance.*)

More.

JUNE. ...June. You. Know my name, too...

> (**BEATRICE** *smiles.*)
>
> (*The two dance.*)
>
> (*The lights change.*)

(**JUNE** *and* **BEATRICE** *dance around the
stage, alternating dance parts.* **JUNE**
twirls **BEATRICE** *and the lights go out when*
BEATRICE *spins.)*

(The sound of giggling.)

(Quiet.)

(Then, the kitchen.)

(**LURIE** *sits reading his newspaper.)*

BEATRICE. In the past three afternoons I've learned all
there is to know about the mambo, the cha-cha, the
samba, *and* the Tango, but I'm just like you, June. The
Tango is surely my favorite. I'm a quick study when it
comes to dancing. I used to watch all Shirley Temple's
movies and teach myself her routines. I could dance the
"Good Ship Lollipop" with almost no mistakes at all.

(To **LURIE.***)* Do you dance, too?

LURIE. Do your parents know where you are?

JUNE. Go back to your paper.

LURIE. You're here every afternoon and every afternoon
you stay until very late.

JUNE. We're having fun, Lurie.

(**JUNE** *and* **BEATRICE** *dance.)*

(**LURIE** *reads.)*

LURIE. ...

        ...

"Bell Curve Proven Accurate: Bussing to Loose Federal
Funds."

BEATRICE. I'm getting good, aren't I?

JUNE. Keep reading.

BEATRICE. I think I am getting very, very good.

LURIE. "Earth moves without being asked: Earthquake strikes tiny island nation." Terrible.

BEATRICE. I'm sure they'll be alright. The island people are Godly people. They'll be fine. I think I am getting very, *very* good.

JUNE. Lurie loves the news. He breathes it.

LURIE. Because the news is pure. Pure possibility. Pure promise. Pure holy matrimony between fact and imagination.

JUNE. Lurie lives in this fantasy world where the news still hold facts.

LURIE. I say there can be both. There is room for all in the news.

JUNE. Circus tent.

LURIE. A man walks into a bank and demands a thousand dollars –

BEATRICE. June, do not give that man one thousand dollars.

JUNE. Well, no. Because I *work* there. I would not steal from there.

BEATRICE. Oh no. Of course not.

JUNE & LURIE & BEATRICE. ...

LURIE. A man walks into a bank and demands a thousand dollars. This is a fact.

Because he needs food? Because he is greedy? Because he craves notoriety?

LURIE. This is imagination. We do not like to call it that, but it is. The reporter and the deed are in constant struggle. Which will win? Which will be fed and which will be devoured and rendered useless? Fact or imagination? One depends on the other and vice versa. The news cannot exist without fact. That is important to know. But the news also cannot exist without imagination. That is vital to know and understand.

BEATRICE. My parents read. They read the Bible. My mother underlines the parts I should know best.

LURIE. Like I said, we'd love to meet her.

BEATRICE. You did not say that.

JUNE. We mean, we don't want them to worry.

BEATRICE. What night is it?

LURIE. Uhhhh, Tuesday?

BEATRICE. Yeah, no, I don't want to go home tonight. Tuna Casserole from Betty Crocker, which my mother got two years ago for Christmas. Tuna Casserole is *not* the most. I'd like to stay. For dinner this time. Please say yes.

LURIE. Check with your –

JUNE. Yes.

LURIE. June.

JUNE. Sure.

BEATRICE. She would let me. And I eat very light. I wouldn't be a burden.

LURIE. June can we talk about –

JUNE. We'd like it.

LURIE. June.

JUNE. Very much.

BEATRICE. I like jam. I like sweet things. If I have jam, I could just have some of that.

LURIE. June.

BEATRICE. Do you have jam?

JUNE. I make it myself.

BEATRICE. OOOOOOOOH. That is the most, June.

JUNE. Raspberry.

BEATRICE. Perfect.

(**LURIE** *signals* **JUNE.**)

LURIE. Pssst.

(**JUNE** *goes to* **LURIE** *behind the newspaper.*)

What exactly is going on with you?

JUNE. What's going on with *you*? Be nice.

LURIE. This is a stranger, June.

JUNE. In a strange land, Lurie. I think her home is not very, not very stable.

Like long dresses, hair in braids, about to be raided by the ATF not stable.

LURIE. Then she sure does not need to set her Prairie Dawn-self up here.

JUNE. Lurie.

LURIE. I am very uncomfortable, June.

JUNE. I feel bad for her.

LURIE. Can you feel bad for her in the public library? Or at Starbucks?

(**JUNE** *turns, goes to a cupboard.*)

JUNE.   I hope we have some jam left. We seem to go
through it so quickly these days.

(JUNE gets a jar of jam from the cupboard.)

(This pleases BEATRICE.)

BEATRICE.   Oh yes, yes, yes.

*(BEATRICE holds out her hands and JUNE
places the jar in BEATRICE's hands. BEATRICE
unscrews the jar and sticks her fingers in. She
licks it.)*

Mmmmm.

(JUNE and LURIE exchange a look.)

JUNE.   Would you? Do you? Want a spoon?

(BEATRICE nods.)

BEATRICE.   Hmm-mmm.

JUNE.   How. How is it? You... You like it?

BEATRICE.   Tops.

LURIE.   You don't say.

JUNE.   Uh. Thanks.

BEATRICE.   Like I've died and gone straight to heaven. No
stopping.

JUNE.   Just jam?

LURIE.   Maybe you want some bread?

(BEATRICE eats.)

Wheat thin?

(BEATRICE eats.)

BEATRICE. My mother used to say all the angels did all day long was sit up in heaven and eat sweet things. If they wanted, that's all they ever had to do.

JUNE. How nice.

BEATRICE. Good girls go straight up to heaven and roll around with the angels

and eat sweet things all day long.

But bad girls.

Bad girls are different.

Nothing ever tastes sweet if you've been a bad girl.

Even if you've only ever been one once,

It's the same as if you've been one a thousand times over.

Nothing ever tastes sweet in your mouth ever.

If you're bad.

If you're wicked.

My mother used to say.

LURIE. Yeah. Um. I uh notice. You keep saying "used to"?

(**JUNE** *jabs* **LURIE** *with her elbow.*)

(**BEATRICE** *yawns big.*)

JUNE. You're tired.

LURIE. Maybe time to go.

BEATRICE. Oh please don't make me do that. Let me stay. Can I stay? Please? For longer than this dinner?

LURIE. It was jam.

BEATRICE. We'd have the most fun. Please, please, please. I will be your most favorite company ever. I can help you with things. I can clean things. I know how real, *real* well. Do you like me? I hope you like me because I like it here. I like it here and I want to stay a long time.

LURIE. A long time? What about your family?

BEATRICE. I'll tell them. They won't mind.

LURIE. June and I will have to discuss –

BEATRICE. Please, please.

LURIE. June and I will have to talk –

JUNE. But I don't see why not.

BEATRICE. OH THANK YOU.

>（**LURIE** *looks at* **JUNE.**）

Tops.

JUNE. We'd love to have you.

BEATRICE. I am so happy. I am so happy I could burst.

JUNE. As long as you'd like.

BEATRICE. Oh, I'd like a long time.

>（*She yawns.*）

But now I'm tired. Could I take a bath?

>（*The sound of water running from a faucet.*）

>（**BEATRICE** *beams at* **JUNE.**）

>（**JUNE** *smiles back.*）

LURIE. *(To himself.)* Used to…

>（*Creeaaaak.*）

>（**JUNE** *and* **BEATRICE** *dance away.*）

>（*Dark.*）

(The sound of metal scraping against glass.)

(The sound of voracious consumption of food.)

(Moonlight through the kitchen window. It reveals **BEATRICE** *eating jam eagerly with the metal spoon. When her spoon can't reach anymore jam, she uses her fingers, licking them as needed, hungrily. She makes small animal like noises.)*

(Lights rise on the kitchen.)

*(**JUNE** in the doorway.)*

JUNE. I'm sorry, I heard noise. I thought it was the house.

*(**BEATRICE** wipes her mouth.)*

BEATRICE. Settling.

JUNE. Right.

BEATRICE. No. Just me. Did I wake you and Lurie up? I'd hate myself if I did that. Lurie. And you too. Need your rest. You've got work, and the party, and – . Just everything, I know.

I hope Lurie is a heavy sleeper.

…

I'm so sorry. It's just so good. So sweet. It's the most.

JUNE. He's a heavy sleeper.

BEATRICE. Looks it.

JUNE. Well. Have all you want. Make yourself right at home.

BEATRICE. Oh thank you. I sure will.

JUNE. Okay.

BEATRICE. Okay.

JUNE. Well. Goodnight then.

BEATRICE. ...

JUNE. ...

BEATRICE. Goodnight.

JUNE. Don't. Stay up too late.

BEATRICE. Do not worry about *me*. I manage. Even when it seems like I hardly have any strength left, even when it seems like I'm just about dead on my feet, I just pop right back to life. Wooosh. I get my second wind.

> (*Clang, clang: pipes.*)

> (**JUNE** *startles.*)

...

JUNE. Okay, well, um: goodnight.

BEATRICE. You too: goodnight.

JUNE. ...

...

> (**JUNE** *looks at* **BEATRICE.**)

> (**JUNE** *can't think of anything else to say.*)

> (*So* **JUNE** *exits.*)

> (**BEATRICE** *watches her, then goes to the cupboard and finds another jar of jam, which she opens and dips into with her metal spoon. She places the spoon in her mouth.*)

> (*Lights down.*)

> (*Creaaaaaak.*)

(Lights up.)

(The kitchen.)

*(**LURIE** and **JUNE**.)*

*(**LURIE** sits at the table reading the paper.)*

(A plastic, lidded container holding meat and marinade sits on the kitchen table.)

*(**LURIE** looks over the corner of his paper at the container. He puts the paper down. He approaches the container, and then gently lifts the lid, leans into the container of meat, and inhales deeply.)*

*(His face is close to the container of meat when **JUNE** enters, laundry basket of towels in her arms.)*

JUNE. Don't bother that meat, Lurie.

LURIE. It looks bloody.

JUNE. I mean it.

LURIE. It looks like there's a lot of blood involved.

JUNE. There isn't. It's marinating.

LURIE. Meat: we're back in the world of the living.

JUNE. Plenty of people do not eat meat.

LURIE. Yes, but when they eat, they do not taste life. When they eat they do not taste something that had life and gave life and can now sustain life. There's something so satisfying about tearing into something that has contained life. Feeling bands of flesh slip against your tongue and slide down your throat. Meat is at its best when it is posthumously seasoned – brought back to enjoy a second livelihood not for the benefit of its former self but for the experience of others – and appreciated not for what it once was – a cow, or pig or some witless chicken – but what it now means to those it serves. Lettuce can never, ever be that powerful.

(**LURIE** *roars like a lion.*)

JUNE. Everyone has to eat that.

(**LURIE** *looks at the towels, which* **JUNE** *has begun folding.*)

LURIE. You're getting awfully friendly.

JUNE. What.

LURIE. Folding towels.

JUNE. She's a guest.

LURIE. If you want to "friend" one of them, friend someone who runs the Garden club. Someone useful.

JUNE. LeRoy's rubbed all up against you.

LURIE. Something is not.

BEATRICE. *(Offstage.)* Ju-une.

JUNE. *(To* **BEATRICE.***)* JUST Ah – . COMING.

LURIE. Coming?

JUNE. *(To* **LURIE.***)* Guest.

LURIE. You don't think it's strange no one's come looking for her? You don't think it's strange she's the only neighbor to coming walking up to our door?

JUNE. She likes it here. And more will come tonight.

LURIE. She doesn't know us. She just *happens to* walk up to us. The only black people for miles. Has she even mentioned when she's leaving? That adoption lady, none of those adoption people at all, are going to like all of a sudden seeing her here.

JUNE. She needs help.

LURIE. Eating jars of jam.

JUNE. We will figure details out later.

LURIE. With her *fingers*. Taking bath after bath running up our hot water.

BEATRICE. *(Offstage.)* JUNE.

JUNE. *(To* **BEATRICE.***)* BE RIGHT THERE.

LURIE. I do not understand your affinity to this urchin-like creature. She hasn't even mentioned when she is leaving.

JUNE. She's very lonely, I think.

LURIE. She's very creepy, I think. Who slips into someone's house and, and, and –

JUNE. Sh. She can probably hear us through the vents. She could have the entire neighborhood talking about us.

LURIE. So that's what this is? Getting a kid to like us so she'll tell the town to like us too?

JUNE. No. no. I –

> *(The doorbell rings.)*

Oh my God.

Oh no, no, no.

They're early?

They're early.

> *(***JUNE** *freaks out.)*

> *(***JUNE** *turns to* **LURIE.***)*

BEATRICE. *(Offstage.)* IT'S COLD UP HERE, JUNE. I NEED YOU.

> *(***JUNE** *turns to* **LURIE***:)*

JUNE. But they're here.

    (**JUNE** *hands* **LURIE** *a stack of folded towels.*)

Could you?

LURIE. Could I what?

JUNE. Stay out of that paper and stop talking about meat and take her a towel? I'll get the door. And I've got so much to do –

LURIE. Take her a towel?

JUNE. *Yes.* Just leave it outside the door.

LURIE. There's a white girl floating around in our bathtub – she's been sitting in there using our hot water all afternoon, when I'm more than sure she's got a perfectly good tub in her own house, with perfectly steaming hot water, meanwhile we don't get to even see the inside of our own bathroom, we don't get to use our own hot water – and you want me to bring her a towel? Do I look like step 'n' fetch it to you?

JUNE. I like her.

LURIE. *Why?*

JUNE. There are people at our front door and that is not what we are discussing.

LURIE. What are we discussing.

JUNE. You helping me. Please. Don't you want everything to go well?

    ...

Then just do this. I'm not in the mood to argue.

    (**JUNE** *goes to exit.*)

And stay away from that meat.

(**LURIE** *leaves the kitchen and heads to the bathroom with the towels.*)

(**BEATRICE** *is the tub, bathing.*)

(**LURIE** *places the towels on the floor, then raps on the door.*)

LURIE. Uh. Here you. Here you go.

BEATRICE. Oh. Thank you.

LURIE. ' welcome.

BEATRICE. Oh, but you're not June, I was calling for June.

LURIE. Company's here. I'll just leave these.

BEATRICE. That's alright. You can come in. You won't look.

LURIE. Aaaaah. No. I'm going to leave these by the door.

BEATRICE. Well I can't reach them if they're by the door, now can I? Wouldn't you like to come in?

LURIE. I'd like to finish my newspaper.

BEATRICE. But I need that towel.

LURIE. And I can leave it right here.

BEATRICE. For a moment come in. To give me that towel. Just a little part of you.

(*Quiet.*)

(*Then...* **LURIE** *slowly backs into the room, folds the towel and places it on the toilet seat.*)

LURIE. (*Back still turned.*) There.

BEATRICE. Thank you.

LURIE. You might want to get dressed. There's company downstairs.

BEATRICE. Oh, but I'll need another bath. I'll need June to come up here.

LURIE. She's busy.

BEATRICE. June runs the baths. She turns on the water for me. It's a very nice thing for her to do.

LURIE. You, you know how to turn on *water*, right? Homeschool's not like *that*? Right?

BEATRICE. I thought you were nice, too.

LURIE. You know how to turn on water.

>   (**LURIE** *smirks.*)

>   (**LURIE** *has called her bluff.*)

>   (**BEATRICE** *smiles.*)

>   (*Bluff called.*)

BEATRICE. I know how to turn on water.

LURIE. Funny.

BEATRICE. Funny. That's me.

LURIE. Well I'll leave you. Company's here. I need to help June.

BEATRICE. That was a lovely bath. I love these baths. I love this entire room. Don't you?

LURIE. Sure.

BEATRICE. I love baths in general. This room in-specific and baths all told in general.

What about you?

LURIE. Sure. I'm heading down.

BEATRICE. Very much? A lot or a little?

>   (**BEATRICE** *begins to prepare for her bath.*)

LURIE. I am definitely heading out.

BEATRICE. You'd definitely like this bath, when it's full. It's lovely, warm.

LURIE. Hope you enjoy yep.

BEATRICE. I bet you'd love this bath very, very much.

LURIE. ...

BEATRICE. You don't think so?

LURIE. I think I should leave you to it.

BEATRICE. I feel most alive when I'm in a bath. It's almost like. I'm. You know. When you put chicken. Or fish in a bowl. Before you cook it. Like that. Before you enjoy it on a plate. Like that.

LURIE. ...

BEATRICE. I'm so happy you and June are letting me stay. I'm a very good house guest, you'll see. And when you and June get your babies, I could play with them, watch over them.

LURIE. June's...shared a lot with you.

BEATRICE. I like June. She's just like a mom. You're lucky.

LURIE. I am.

BEATRICE. She's lucky.

LURIE. Thank you. Welp. You've got towels. You know how to work a faucet.

BEATRICE. You've been married six long years or six short years?

LURIE. Good years. Six good years.

BEATRICE. That's very sweet. Aren't you super sweet. I hope when I grow up I have someone just as sweet. For now, I have my baths. So wonderful. Here: see for yourself.

LURIE. I'm gonna see who was at the door.

BEATRICE. See for yourself.

LURIE. And it needs to fill back up.

BEATRICE. No. Look. Filled.

>   (**LURIE** *peers in the tub.*)

>   (*The sound of water lapping.*)

>   (*Steam hangs in the air.*)

>   (**LURIE** *looks at the faucet.*)

LURIE. Um.

BEATRICE. Feel for yourself.

LURIE. Wait. Uh...

BEATRICE. How about your elbow. That's not all of you. It's just a little bit of you.

LURIE. Elbow...

BEATRICE. Roll up your sleeve.

>   (**LURIE** *looks at his sleeve.*)

Aren't you curious?

This tub is filled.

Don't be a baby.

One elbow.

Just one elbow.

Is that so much?

You'll like it in here.

In here it feels most alone.

You like the world of the living.

I do too.

And that's what it's like here in my bath.

... Are you shy? You're shy. You're embarrassed.

I won't look. I won't even look. I'll turn right around.

But you're curious.

I can tell.

> (**LURIE** *looks at the tub.*)

> (**LURIE** *looks at the steam.*)

> (**LURIE** *looks back at the tub.*)

> (*Then.*)

> (**LURIE** *unbuttons the wrist of his shirt. He rolls up his sleeve. And he begins to walk towards the tub. When he is about the touch the water in the tub,* **BEATRICE** *reaches out –.*)

Not with that. Like I said. With this.

> (**BEATRICE** *points to her own elbow.* **LURIE** *looks down at his elbow. He lowers it into the tub, then jumps back.*)

LURIE. OW.

BEATRICE. Hot. Yes? Here.

> (**BEATRICE** *beckons to him. He steps towards her.* **BEATRICE** *gently lowers and sucks on his elbow.*)

Better?

LURIE. Ah, um. We have company –

BEATRICE. Coming?

LURIE. I should go see, go help.

BEATRICE. June.

LURIE. I don't help enough.

BEATRICE. No, no / you've done a great job with the house.

LEROY. You've done a great job with the house.

(*The kitchen.*)

(**JUNE** *and* **LEROY.**)

JUNE. Well I did want you all to see it.

LEROY. What, I don't count?

JUNE. Tasha. The kids.

LEROY. It's a ways out.

JUNE. She said she was coming.

LEROY. Next time.

JUNE. On the group text you all all said –

LEROY. Well where's *your* people, you so nosy. Where's my big brother?

Finding more ways to make the value of this property sink like a lead weight?

JUNE. What? What's that mean?

LEROY. You can't cement shit, June.

JUNE. Cement?

LEROY. The floor. In the bathroom. Next time call me. I know people. I will call people.

Better yet. I'll fix it myself.

JUNE. ...

It *was* nice for you to do the pipes. In time for the party. Lurie's probably got his nose in a paper somewhere.

LEROY. It's going to be okay, June.

JUNE. Back porch, or...

LEROY. All this is going to work.

JUNE. I'm gonna text him…

LEROY. It's just going to take time –

JUNE.   HonestlyLuriebreathesthatpaper "didweget thepaper""I'mgettingthepaper""Babe, gotthepaper" likeanoldmanwearestillyoungItellhimweare notoldI'dliketotakethatpaperandtearit intolittleshredsIdonotfeelikeIhavetimeIwant itallnowtodayYouandTashaareverylucky. Four.Beautiful.

Thanks for driving out.

LEROY. Lurie thinks burying his head in that newspaper's going to keep the past from creeping around. That is my verdict. But you can't just bury the past. You bury it, and any way it can it's going to rise up and live again. Any way it can it's going to make you work twice as hard to try and beat it back down and bury it again. The newspaper's Lurie's way of not having to look at anything that's right in front of his face. You. That baby. Waiting and waiting for another chance. But the past always comes creeping back around. It's always there. That paper's *proof* it's always there. It's proof *now* did not come from out of nowhere.

The past breeds the present. The present breeds the answer, if we listen. And they can't get away from each other. They're parent and child. How far away can a child really get away from its parent?

…

…

> (**JUNE** *looks at* **LEROY**.)

> (**LEROY** *looks at* **JUNE**.)

She'll always be right here.

*(**LEROY** taps where **JUNE***'s heart rests.)*

LEROY. You're looking sad.

JUNE. I just think Lurie can do more than type Bill Blake's words. That's why his head shouldn't be stuffed behind that paper. And the pay would –

*(**JUNE** looks at **LEROY**.)*

LEROY. We can't all bring home the bacon, fry it, serve it, dance the Foxtrot around it.

JUNE. There is no bacon. This house has taken all my bacon.

LEROY. You're looking so sad. I told you Lurie would mess this all up. Should have picked me, June.

JUNE. You go in and see where Lurie is. I've got all this food to get out.

*(**LEROY** holds out his arms.)*

LEROY. Old times sake. So I don't look sad, too.

*(**JUNE** looks at **LEROY**.)*

*(**JUNE** raises her hands to **LEROY**.)*

(They dance.)

(Creaaaaak.)

(The bathroom.)

*(**BEATRICE** and **LURIE** as before.)*

BEATRICE. – A great job with the house.**

Absolutely.

LURIE. Thanks.

BEATRICE. I even love that you moved the tub.

Gosh I'm cold.

I am just shivering.

I've got goosebumps.

Look.

Look.

Little hills on my skin just getting harder and harder.

I need a towel.

…

…

…

…

> (*Finally,* **LURIE** *reaches for a towel and hands it to* **BEATRICE**.)

Can you tell? I have goosebumps?

> (**LURIE** *holds out the towel.*)

> (**BEATRICE** *smiles.*)

> (**BEATRICE** *waits for* **LURIE** *to place the towel in her hand.*)

> (*He does.*)

> (*She smiles.*)

I think you're the first real friends I've ever had that I'm going to get to keep.

LURIE. Keep?

BEATRICE. You're a good friend, a great friend. Look, you've kept me warm.

> (*She steps towards him and he steps back.*)

Don't be frightened, Lurie, I'll keep you.

LURIE. Beatrice –

BEATRICE. Don't worry about that one bit. Cross my heart, hope to die, stick a needle in my eye. Dance?

LURIE. Dance? Now? Here?

BEATRICE. Yes now here. You dance with June all the time.

LURIE. She's. My wife.

BEATRICE. I'm your friend.

LURIE. No. No, no, no.

BEATRICE. This is making me upset.

LURIE. Let's see who was at the door.

BEATRICE. It's a party. Anybody can be at the door, but I'm up here now. The earth moves without being asked, Lurie, so should you.

>   (**BEATRICE** *holds up her arms.*)
>
>   (**LURIE** *looks at* **BEATRICE.**)
>
>   (**LURIE** *complies.*)
>
>   (*They dance.*)
>
>   (*The two couples dance around the space.*)
>
>   (*The lights change.*)
>
>   (*The couples almost collide.*)
>
>   (*Right before* **LURIE** *and* **JUNE**'s *backs collide, they turn to each other.*)
>
>   (*The kitchen, now littered with too much left over from the party.*)
>
>   (**BEATRICE** *and* **LEROY** *exit.*)

LURIE. That girl has to go.

JUNE. Nobody came.

LURIE. June. Listen. Please.

JUNE. The new neighbors, even your mother and Tasha and the kids...

LURIE. We don't know her. There's something off about her.

JUNE. Beatrice is the only one to stop by, to be friendly.

LURIE. Friendly. Yeah. Uh. She. She has ideas, June –

JUNE. I told you, her family is completely warped. She uses the word "Negro." She's. Yes. Off. But she's a nice girl.

LURIE. No, I don't think she *is* a nice girl. If we had kids and they went to school with someone like her –

JUNE. That's the thing. Her parents yanked her *out* of school. What would we be like if our parents yanked us out of school?

LURIE. This is not homeschool this is Netflix binge watch shit.

JUNE. She's a good girl.

LURIE. To be good you have to come from good, and I do not think that is the *case*. Here. I do not believe –

JUNE. Take a look around. We paid to live in the middle of good.

LURIE. The middle of good and white are not the same thing.

JUNE. I did not say that, when did I say that, you are saying that. Good roads, good schools, good families. I did not say white.

LURIE. If everything is so good how come we found some dead person in our bathroom?

JUNE. We should not have used cement, LeRoy would not shut up about it tonight.

LURIE. You tell me how all that happened in the bathroom, if we are in the middle of good.

JUNE. I don't want to think about what happened. That was a long time ago.

LURIE. I think, I think, I think maybe there was, is, not, so much good here. I think someone who buries somebody in their bathroom is not so good. I think, whatever is going on with that girl, is not so good.

JUNE. We did not come this far to, to, to... You think, you think, you think: too much.

You are ruining everything, Lurie. I have waited too long. My mother –

LURIE. Things were rough. Things have been very. Rough. For you. But what kind of people are we if we can live in this house with something like that, crumpled in under the floor.

JUNE. Sh.

LURIE. What kind of people –

JUNE. We are good, we are still good people. Who want good things, who deserve good things, whose chances are, whose chances are... Can't you feel them getting smaller and smaller? Don't, Lurie, don't go ruining our chances for good things. Keep all that quiet. Don't talk about it, don't think about it –

LURIE. We sell this house. We go someplace we know. Where there isn't danger, June. I feel danger, here –

(**JUNE** *covers* **LURIE**'s *mouth with her hand.*)

JUNE. Don't talk about it, don't think about it, just push it all down somewhere deep, deep inside you. Close your eyes and hold your breath and push: push very,

very hard. Just let it sink down so far you won't be able to find it anywhere ever. Let it disappear down there. Let it go. Why? Because we are good people and we deserve good things.

> (**LURIE** *grabs* **JUNE**'s *wrist and removes* **JUNE**'s *hand from his mouth.*)

LURIE. Find out where she comes from. I don't think it's a good place.

> (*Creaaaaak.*)

> (*The kitchen.*)

> (*The food that was intended for the housewarming sits on the table, uneaten.*)

> (**LURIE** *sits behind his paper.*)

> (**JUNE** *and* **BEATRICE** *sit.*)

> (**BEATRICE** *looks around at the kitchen.*)

> (**BEATRICE** *smiles at* **LURIE** *but* **LURIE** *retreats behind his paper.*)

BEATRICE. You've got a lot left over. But day-old food isn't so bad, but. You should have RSVP'd. Next time, have the invitation RSVP. Maybe then someone will show up.

LURIE. We'll remember that.

JUNE. It's summer. People are busy.

BEATRICE. Maybe.

I'm thirsty.

JUNE. Water?

BEATRICE. Milk. Please.

> (**JUNE** *gets the milk.*)

JUNE. ...

Well, drink up.

BEATRICE. But the Petersons never go anywhere. And the Richardsons only go skiing. So. It might just be you.

JUNE. Thank you, Beatrice.

BEATRICE. I like to be helpful.

JUNE. Sure.

BEATRICE. I like to be truthful.

JUNE. Sure, sure. There's just. A delicacy. An art. To communication.

    (**BEATRICE** *blinks at* **JUNE.**)

One should strive to be truthful, but also: kind.

BEATRICE. Well I don't know about that. Sometimes the person you're talking to just doesn't know better. Then you're letting them stay stupid. I think that's what my father might say.

He's wrong a lot, but I think this time he'd be right.

JUNE. Your father, your parents, have a lot of ideas.

BEATRICE. ...They do.

JUNE. Living with them, sounds difficult.

BEATRICE. ...

    ...

JUNE. We're just wondering, Beatrice, about them, about your parents, since you've been here a while now.

    (**LURIE** *peers at* **JUNE** *and* **BEATRICE** *from behind his newspaper.*)

BEATRICE. You don't want me here?

JUNE. No, no, I didn't say that –

BEATRICE. Lurie doesn't want me here?

(**LURIE** *goes back behind the paper.*)

JUNE. I'm worried about your parents.

BEATRICE. Why are you worried about them?

JUNE. They don't miss you?

BEATRICE. Don't push me.

JUNE. No, no, we're not –

BEATRICE. You can't make me do anything I don't want to do, because I know things about this house.

(**LURIE** *stays behind his paper.*)

And I know things about you.

(**LURIE** *peers from behind his paper.*)

(*Throughout,* **BEATRICE** *pokes her fingers in the jars of jam and licks as much as she can from her fingers.*)

JUNE. Let's just tell someone where you are. Then you can stay and things will be fine.

BEATRICE. I know about cement. I know what you did.

JUNE & LURIE. ...

...

JUNE. I'm not sure we understand what you're talking about.

BEATRICE. Don't lie.

JUNE. We're not. I think you are. And we are. Confused. I just don't think we understand –

BEATRICE. I say you do. You tried to kill me.

JUNE. We did not.

BEATRICE. You did, you did, you did.

> *(The house rattles.)*

And you almost got away with it.

(To **LURIE.***)* You know, Lurie. You were there. You saw how she wanted to seal me up underneath all that cement.

> *(***LURIE** *and* **JUNE** *begin to move away from* **BEATRICE.***)*

(To **JUNE.***)* You wanted to trap me in there just like my mother did. But I got out.

JUNE. Ooooooo.

LURIE. Shhhhhh.

BEATRICE. I live here.

JUNE. Oh God.

BEATRICE. But. I am happy you moved in. I am happy you joined me.

> *(***LURIE** *tries the kitchen door, but it does not open.)*

I like Negroes. (And I really don't see what's wrong with that name, June, if I say it like that, with love, like that.) I'd never met any Negroes I got to keep.

LURIE. Keep?

JUNE. *(To* **LURIE.***)* Open that door.

LURIE. *(To* **JUNE.***)* It won't –

BEATRICE. Well.

There was one before I stopped going to school.

But I wasn't allowed to keep her at all.

Virginia.

She was a Negro.

She was my first friend.

I wanted to invite her over and bake her cookies

I wanted to keep her all to myself.

I wanted my mother to stay up in her room with her Bible.

But Virginia kept making me laugh.

Virginia was very funny.

I dribbled milk all down the front of my dress, I laughed so much.

I laughed so much, my mother heard.

And she took one look at Virginia and her eyes nearly exploded out of her head.

And she walked right back up the stairs and down the hall to her room.

> *(We hear footsteps overhead, loud, we hear a door creeaaak open, then we hear footsteps again, moving closer and closer to us...)*

I tried to get Virginia to leave.

But she wouldn't move, she didn't understand.

Virginia didn't have a mother, she told me once under the bushes at recess in my ear.

She doesn't understand what one can be like if your father likes you better.

> *(The footsteps stop at the interior kitchen doorway, and **BEATRICE** turns sharply in the doorway's direction.)*

BEATRICE. My mother walked into the kitchen and sat at the table.

She opened her book and set it flat under Virginia's chin.

She read out loud before either of us could speak.

"Cursed be Canaan: a servant of servants shall he be unto his brethren.

Blessed by the Lord God of Shem:

And Canaan shall be his servant."

And Virginia, she didn't know what to do.

But I did.

> (**BEATRICE** *bows her head and recites.*)

"Cursed be Canaan: a servant of servants…"

And my mother pointed at me and said:

"And Ham, the father of Canaan saw the nakedness of his father,

And told his two brethren without.

And Shem and Ja-pheth took a garment and laid it upon both their shoulders,

And went backward and covered the nakedness of their father;

And their faces were backward and they saw not their father's nakedness."

I pinched my eyes closed, way closed:

Theysawnottheirfather'snakednessTheysawnottheirfather'snakedness.Theysawnottheirfather's –

When I opened my eyes Virginia was gone.

Her glass of milk spilled out on the table.

A sloppy puddle on the floor.

"She only had to spend two minutes in your father's house,"

My mother said.

"And now look: It's not clean. And neither. Are you."

So I got a sponge.

I cleaned the floor.

> (*The sound of feet climbing stairs, walking back down a hall, and a door creaaaaking open once more...*)

My mother doesn't like niggers.

I don't use that word ever, June, but she does.

I know not to.

She *and* my father say they're dirty

And they steal

And where they come from is even dirtier than they themselves are

And they all have that bad man named Ham for a relative.

I don't think that.

I know that's not true, because Ham's son Canaan and me are alike.

My mother told me.

And I don't steal and I am very, very clean. I keep myself that way on purpose.

Virginia never came over after school again.

But that was a very long time ago. My mother's dead now.

And I can stay down here and have friends as long as I want.

BEATRICE. Maybe for a short time, maybe for a long time.

Ghosts are like this you know. Very temperamental.

This is not your house. It's my father's house. If you earn it, I'll let you have it.

JUNE. Earn it? Now listen –

BEATRICE. GRRRRRR.

(*Slam – an upstairs door.*)

See? See what I can do? See what I've been doing all along?

LURIE. Shhhiiit.

BEATRICE. Oh Lurie. So sweet.

(**JUNE** *looks to* **LURIE.**)

LURIE. (*To* **JUNE.**) Shhh-sh. It will all be okay.

BEATRICE. Oh, it will.

Don't worry.

Are you worried?

Don't be worried.

I'm going to help you have it.

It's going to be my good deed.

It's going to help me get into heaven.

I'm going to help you to take care of this house the way it should be taken care of

(The people after my parents really let things *go*), and so I am going to help you earn it.

After I do, I'll be ready.

After I do, heaven will want me.

So you will help me get ready, and I will help you have this house.

Because.

Because you love this house.

And you need this house if you're going to have children.

The adoption lady won't give them to you

If you don't have a nice home like I did for children to grow up in.

So.

I need to keep clean and the house will have to be kept clean.

I'll need lots of towels and they should be snow white and...and smell like lilacs.

Fresh lilacs.

I need Jesus to let me in and Jesus only wants clean people.

And...let's see...what else?

Jam.

I like to eat sweet things. To eat. I like this jam and you'll make more for me.

Also, I've decided I like dancing.

You and I danced, Lurie –

>   (**JUNE** *looks to* **LURIE** *again.*)

>   (**LURIE** *looks down.*)

BEATRICE. And I liked it very much.

So you'll dance with me, when I ask.

Annnnd... I need lots of rest.

Being around again takes up a lot of my energy.

BEATRICE. Especially after I eat, eating takes up the most.

And I will need to rest in my special place, the place where you found me.

So the cement has to go, it has to leave.

LURIE. The floor.

BEATRICE. Yes, the floor. Beeswax in your ears, silly.

JUNE. Dig it up.

BEATRICE. *Fix* the floor, not dig it up. Did I say dig? Fix, because you ruined it. The cement has to go because you ruined it. That is where I rest the best. That is where my mother put me. And I can hear things that way. I can hear you breathe that way.

(To **JUNE.***)* And you can hear me breathe that way. I know you can. You said it yourself.

If I were very truthful, I would admit, I would not like to sleep in the floor.

But that is where I rest best. That is where my mother left me.

So. Uh. Yes. We're agreed. We've made a deal.

JUNE. Beatrice.

BEATRICE. We. Have made. A deal.

(Rattle.)

Or you won't get this house. The cement has to go.

JUNE. ...

... The cement has to go.

*(***BEATRICE** *then turns to* **LURIE** *...)*

LURIE. The cement has to go.

BEATRICE. And you will do all these things.

(**JUNE** *and* **LURIE** *look at each other.*)

Or I will not be able to ever leave, ever get to heaven,

Where I belong,

And I might be forced to wreck parts of my father's beautiful house.

I wouldn't want to.

And you want those babies; your family.

JUNE. Yes. We do.

BEATRICE. So promise to be nice.

(*Creaaaaaak.*)

(*Lights go down.*)

(*Rest.*)

(*Rest.*)

(*Rest.*)

(*A break can be taken here if needed.*)

(*In darkness the sound of heavy breathing, then scraping, then both. The two sounds become more frantic. The scraping blends and bleeds into the sound of digging and then the grating of pieces of broken tile rubbing against each other.*)

(*Silence.*)

(*Lights rise on* **JUNE** *and* **LURIE** *in the bathroom. A hammer and broken tile litter the space.*)

JUNE. Nothing. There's –

LURIE. Nothing.

JUNE. You try.

LURIE. June –

JUNE. Dig.

LURIE. There's nothing.

JUNE. Maybe deeper down there's something. She has to be somewhere.

LURIE. If she is, then who's downstairs?

JUNE. Dig.

LURIE. I've got it. She's the undead. Zombie. This is it. This is the apocalypse. Mandy Suarez did an exposé on this last year. I captioned the whole thing I know all about it.

JUNE. Mandy also did an exposé on dryer lint.

LURIE. Highly flammable. We're all going to die.

JUNE. So she is not going to be our go-to on how to get this girl out of my kitchen.

LURIE. Let's. Keep our voices down.

　　　　　(**JUNE** *looks at* **LURIE.**)

She can hear us. She said.

JUNE. She said, yeah, a whole lot of things.

LURIE. Canaan. Ham?

JUNE. Dancing.

　　　　　(**LURIE** *looks at* **JUNE.**)

LURIE. If we're nice to her, she'll go away.

JUNE. That is our strategy *now*. Before, I just asked you to –

LURIE. To be *nice*.

JUNE. She seemed cozy.

LURIE. I was happy where I could get a roti and a haircut on the same block but here we are.

JUNE. What are you talking about?

LURIE. I told you she was no good.

JUNE. So you go get down with her in some corner of the house –

LURIE. What are *you* talking about?

JUNE. It's what she, what *she* was talking about. "We danced Lurie, and I liked that very much." Like what the hell? Like when was this?

LURIE. *You told me to be nice.*

JUNE. You know what? Just. Just. She has to be in here somewhere.

(She begins to dig with her hands.)

She-has-to-be-in-here-somewhere –

(She digs fiercely then collapses amidst the piles of debris.)

BEATRICE. *(Offstage.)* JU-NE.

Ju-une?

(Neither **JUNE** *nor* **LURIE** *move.)*

June?

BEATRICE. Lurie?

Come feed me. I'm hungry.

(The house rattles.)

I said I'm *hungry*.

LURIE. We should –

> (**JUNE** *resumes digging.*)

JUNE. This is my houseThis is my houseThis is my house.

> (*She curls into the floor, exhausted, chanting...*)
>
> (*The sound of knuckles banging against a glass door.*)
>
> (*The kitchen.*)
>
> (*A shadow can be seen on the far side of the door.*)
>
> (**BEATRICE** *sits at the table, empty jam jar nearby.*)

LEROY. (*From other side of the door.*) Lurie? June? Anybody home?

> (**LEROY** *tries to open the door, but it doesn't budge.*)

It's me. LeRoy to fix the floor.

> (**BEATRICE** *cocks her head, but otherwise does not move.*)
>
> (*Still, still...the shadow retreats...*)
>
> (**LURIE** *enters from the interior of the house.*)

BEATRICE. I'm hungry.

LURIE. I thought I heard.

BEATRICE. I need more jam.

> (**LURIE** *is about to open the back kitchen door...*)

I need more jam, *now.*

>(*The kitchen door rattles.*)

>(**LURIE** *regards the door.*)

LURIE. Jam...

BEATRICE. In the cupboard.

>(**LURIE** *goes to the cupboard.*)

LURIE. We're...all out...

BEATRICE. Well this is not good.

LURIE. But I can get some.

BEATRICE. You'd do that for me? How sweet, Lurie, honestly. You're the most, I swear you are. Even though I would rather it not be store bought. You've made me so happy I, I feel like *dancing.*

LURIE. I can go to the store, and be back with raspberry jam in no time at all.

BEATRICE. No: Dance. I said I want to and you are supposed to do what I ask. Honestly Lurie I don't understand you. We were having a perfectly wonderful time before. You brought me that towel. We danced.

LURIE. You can't bring that up whenever it pops in your mind.

BEATRICE. But it was so wonderful. Just like Shirley on those movies on TV. The Blacks in those movies are very nice to Shirley. They think she's the most. Why can't you be like that?

LURIE. Because those are just movies.

BEATRICE. That doesn't mean they're not real.

LURIE. Someone writes them. Someone makes them up, then writes them. Someone makes Shirley Temple and whoever else is in those movies with her friends on paper first.

BEATRICE. Well a little bit of it has to be real. Or else how could they put it into a movie and expect people to come to that movie and want to see that movie again and again?

A little bit of it has to be real or else the whole thing wouldn't work at all, now would it? And the people who see it think it's real, so what's the difference if it's only real on paper first?

LURIE. The people who write those movies want you to think it's real, but it isn't. It never was.

BEATRICE. How do you know never?

LURIE. The people who write those movies make things up that they think people will want to see. So that they'll make money. It doesn't ever have to be real.

BEATRICE. But a little part of it has to be.

LURIE. They just have to be able to sell it. After that, nothing matters at all.

BEATRICE. Well what does that have to do with Shirley Temple, Mr. Smarty?

LURIE. When those movies were made – . It's different now, but when those movies where made, people liked seeing a pretty, curly haired girl dance around with a nice old uncle. It didn't make them scared. It made them happy.

BEATRICE. What kind of American isn't happy to see Shirley Temple? Pinko commies, that's who.

LURIE. That little girl and that old man were not friends. They were not happy together.

Not really.

BEATRICE. Yes sir they were. He bought here a car. A real little car in real life.

I read that in my uncle's wife's magazine she kept under her mattress. It had a real engine and rubber tires. Now why would he do that if he didn't really like her?

LURIE. I'm talking about the movies.

BEATRICE. I'm talking about much more. I've given this a lot of thought, Lurie, and I've come up with answers. Shirley and those Blacks wouldn't be able to sing and dance around with each other if a little part of them didn't like the other person. Just a little part.

That's enough to be real in my book.

LURIE. I don't feel. Much like dancing. This is. This is very hard for us, Beatrice. No matter what it seems our outside says.

BEATRICE. But I would like to dance. Right now. You're just like that pot roast you wanted, that pot roast for that party you should have made everyone RSVP for.

I've got to chew and chew you until you slide around and down into me.

Right now you're useless if you do what I say, if you won't dance with me.

LURIE. I don't think –

BEATRICE. I didn't ask you to think I asked you to dance. Shirley Temple didn't have to deal with this crap. Don't think, just *do*. No wonder June gets so mad at you all the time. You're no good if you won't slide into me like jam, and you're certainly not nice to me if you're willing to make me so angry, so angry I, I, I, just want to –

(The sound of glass breaking.)

*(**JUNE** enters.)*

JUNE. What in the world?

LURIE. June, she –

BEATRICE. I was very angry. Lurie made me that way.

JUNE. We just want to get through this in one piece.

LURIE. I know, I know. But –

BEATRICE. Man oh man, Lurie can be stubborn sometimes.

JUNE. Let's. Just get through this.

> (**JUNE** *looks at* **LURIE.**)

LURIE. We're out of jam. I'm gonna get more jam.

BEATRICE. I *tried* to tell him I didn't want to dance. I *tried*, June, but Lurie's so stubborn and so even though I tried to talk to him,

To talk him out of it –

LURIE. What? No.

BEATRICE. He just –

LURIE. June.

JUNE. One piece.

BEATRICE. I should probably just dance with you June anyway. If you don't mind. It wouldn't look right for me to dance with Lurie. I mean alone and everything. How would it look? Not very good. Not very good at all for Lurie to touch me that way. Look how much bigger he is than me. Honestly, how, how does it all *look*?

LURIE. To who? Who is in here? No one's in here. Just us in here. We're alone.

Completely alone.

(To **JUNE.**) I never wanted this. We don't need to do this. Look what is happening. It's me. It's Lurie. I would never. I would never. Listen to what she is saying. June, come on.

> (**BEATRICE** *yawns loudly.*)

BEATRICE. I do need some more jam. Yours is so good. Don't bother with that store. I won't like it. Now: a bath.

> (**BEATRICE** *exits.*)

LURIE. June.

JUNE. Just do what she says.

LURIE. *June*, baby –

JUNE. We are so close, we are so close. We have worked so hard –

LURIE. We can pack the car. Take a trip. Go far away –

JUNE. *She* needs to go away *first*. A ghost can't live here with us.

LURIE. I... I don't think she *is* a ghost. Ghosts haunt. They come back to specific places, they relive past moments –

JUNE. Then everyone is haunted. What? So *I'm* haunted? I'd give anything to be haunted.

I'd give anything for

one more minute;

one more bath;

one more kiss on the cheek;

one more button on the sleeper;

one more check of the milk on my wrist;

one more smell of her hair,

one more, one more, one more.

JUNE. But she is not here.

So I am not.

I am not haunted.

(**LURIE** *pulls* **JUNE** *to him.*)

JUNE. I am not, I am not, I am not.

LURIE. I miss her too... But. We need to leave.

JUNE. I can't.

...This. This is our house.

LURIE. I know it's hard. Baby, I know it's so, so hard. But we can, we *can* leave. I will *help* us leave. Okay? Okay? It's going to be okay... Seee, see, that's the. That is the difference between us and Beatrice. And when I think about it. When I really think about it. I don't even think Beatrice is a normal ghost. Ghosts are supposed to choose a moment they've lived, and only live that one moment, over and over again. If we are truly living, truly living, we have the ability to reshape our moments, we have the ability to see ourselves as a continuum of moments. We are not one or two, we're many. We can hold more than one reality in our minds at once –

BEATRICE. *(Offstage.)* JU-UNE, I'm Co-old.

(**LURIE** *and* **JUNE** *look up.*)

(**LURIE** *looks at* **JUNE**, *takes* **JUNE** *in.*)

LURIE. And you and me, we are more than whatever Beatrice's moment has us trapped inside, we are more than those moments that almost tore our hearts out. *June* –

(**LURIE** *looks at* **JUNE**.)

BEATRICE. *(Offstage.)* JUNE.

LURIE. I don't think Beatrice is haunting us. I think she's living with us, trying to live with us, not really haunt us, but *live* with us, to correct some moment? one moment? some one thing: but I say let's just leave, let's –

JUNE. No, I want *her* gone. Away from my house, away from my husband.

LURIE. She's nowhere near me.

    (**LURIE** *looks at* **JUNE.**)

BEATRICE. *(Offstage.)* JU-UNE, I need a To-wel. Or I will catch the Asiatic Fl-u.

    (**JUNE** *enters the bathroom with towels.*)

    (*Lights down on the kitchen.*)

And that is one of the worst kind of flu, you know. Those orientals: Yeesh.

JUNE. We don't. Call the flu that anymore. We name it after numbers and birds and pigs.

BEATRICE. If I were to die of that I'd hope people would bring me lilacs tied with ribbon.

Virginia did that once.

She used a beautiful yellow ribbon and I put them on my window sill in my room.

They shriveled into brown crisps.

I cut that ribbon into strips, thin, thin strips, and then I braided my hair into pig-tails –

All over my head I had pig-tails –

And I decorated them with that yellow ribbon and looked just like Virginia, I thought.

When my mother saw me, Oh boy.

BEATRICE. Jiminy Cricket she yanked those yellow bows off my head so fast

She pulled out some of my hair.

Then she burned them.

Took a match and poof up they went.

If you have a little girl, if that's what they give you, you can braid her hair all over her head.

Like Virginia.

JUNE. ...

...

We don't mind boy or girl.

BEATRICE. Those lilacs were awfully nice.

JUNE. Did you ever. Give Virginia anything? To be nice back?

(**BEATRICE** *blinks.*)

She seems so kind, did you ever return the favor?

BEATRICE. I...had a set of jacks.

I could have given those to her if I –

Those cookies.

And that milk.

You are trying to trick me, June.

But I'm too quick.

Oh, you'll make a great mother.

You'll be lots of fun.

They'll bring a baby for sure.

They'll find one and bring it right here.

My father says the blacks have the most babies out of everyone.

That's what's wrong with the South.

That's what's wrong with most places that aren't American.

Too many people having too many babies.

There isn't enough hot water to go around.

JUNE. That's not a very nice thing to say, Beatrice.

BEATRICE. Oh, but he didn't know about blacks like you. Lurie writes, and people let you touch their money. And none of the blacks my father knew ever did any of those things. So, he didn't mean blacks like you. Don't feel bad. Do you feel bad?

JUNE. People nowadays don't say the kinds of things your father said.

BEATRICE. Not out loud.

JUNE. Or when they do, they. They don't say them quite like that. To people's faces the way you keep doing.

BEATRICE. But I'm your *friend*. If I wasn't your friend I wouldn't even think of letting you have this house for your babies. You'd better start remembering how much you want this house. It's very important you have it, isn't it?

JUNE. Because it's the one we bought.

BEATRICE. But it's very important you have *this* house

And not some other one is some other place, isn't it?

JUNE. This is just where the house happened to be.

BEATRICE. But it wouldn't be right to live someplace dirty, would it?

JUNE. Well no one wants to live someplace dirty.

BEATRICE. Exactly nobody is my guess.

Shirley Temple was very clean in her movies.

I think Shirley Temple's mother must have worked very hard to keep her very shiny.

My mother says Shirley Temple was so clean that standing next to the coloreds,

Tapping around like that made Shirley Temple

look like the cleanest little girl in the whole wide world.

She also said Shirley Temple's mother worked hard to keep her that way.

My mother worked just as hard trying to keep me that clean.

But it was harder, because I was wicked.

When Shirley Temple dies, my mother always said, she will go straight to heaven.

And tap, tap, tap around and will eat sweet things with the angels

And will stay so squeaky clean up there that you will be able to see your reflection in her forehead.

But that will be a sad day, when Shirley dies.

JUNE. I have news for you. That day's come, Beatrice.

BEATRICE. That. Is. *Awful.*

I guess a lot's changed since I've been sealed up.

JUNE. Well, you've got fresh towels now.

(**JUNE** *turns to leave.*)

BEATRICE. It *would* be terrible if you didn't have this house. I'm right. That's why you need to stay here.

JUNE. You need more jam.

BEATRICE. And you like it here.

JUNE. You need more jam.

BEATRICE. It's nice and clean –

JUNE. I'll start on some.

BEATRICE. You know, I don't think you're very different from my parents. Not at all.

The difference is my father says things out loud that you think inside.

JUNE. I am nothing like your father.

BEATRICE. My parents bought this house because it is in a good place. The people here are clean and good, and that other place, wherever you came from, has other kind of people that aren't so good.

JUNE. That is not true.

BEATRICE. Then why are you here? If those other people are not bad, bad, bad to the bone?

JUNE. This is where the house happened to be.

BEATRICE. A little bitty part of you wants this house for yourself. You're a good person. You've said so yourself. And you deserve nice things.

JUNE. Our children –

BEATRICE. You don't care about children. You care about you.

JUNE. Be quiet.

BEATRICE. You want this house. You want this house for you. I know I'm right. I've watched. I've listened.

JUNE. You do not know me.

BEATRICE. Oh yes I do. I know you are trying to get this house when you haven't earned it.

JUNE. Oh yes. Yes I have.

BEATRICE. No. No, you are lazy. You are selfish and you are lazy just like your mother.

JUNE. What did you just say to me?

BEATRICE. Maybe if your mother had scrubbed a few more floors –

JUNE. I said be quiet –

BEATRICE. Washed a few more dishes –

JUNE. QUIET.

BEATRICE. *You* could have come from someplace good, too.

If your mother hadn't been like all those other blacks,

Then while you were still a little a very little girl

You could have been kept very clean and very safe all the time.

You work and you work

And it's not for those *babies*,

You want to be clean.

Deep, deep down for the first time in your life.

And Lurie wouldn't help you if he knew this was all just for you.

Every waking moment you think of being *un*clean and *un*safe.

And that's not the present at all.

That's the past.

JUNE. I said shut *up*.

BEATRICE. Maybe if your mother had let some crinkly man lift her skirt a few more times –

> (**JUNE** *lunges for* **BEATRICE. BEATRICE** *squirms out of the way but* **JUNE***'s body hits*

the tub faucet and a loud shrill whine is heard from one of the pipes.)

Ohhhh.

> (**BEATRICE** *holds her head.)*

OHHHHHHHH.

> (**BEATRICE** *reaches for the faucet, she manages to turn it off, and moans during the quiet that follows.)*

Too much noise is not good for me. I... I can't think clearly when –

> (**JUNE** *turns the faucet.)*

> (*Shrill whines fill the room.)*

JUNE. You mean like this?

BEATRICE. *Stop that.*

> *GRRRRR.*

> (*Lightening.)*

> (*Thunder.)*

> (**JUNE** *looks up, frightened.)*

> (**JUNE** *turns off the faucet.)*

Now you listen to me.

You think you can work a little extra and just take over where someone is *living*?

I *earned* this house.

Every day my mother would cram me full of her rules and then

Every night my father would push his rules into me –

Every single night of my whole ENTIRE life –

BEATRICE. I earned this house and I'll rot in hell before I just give it up

to the first person who waltzes in off the streets.

I spent sixteen years obeying

And now it's my turn to be the one making the rules.

Everything will work out if you just do what I say, June.

You'll get this house and you'll be safe and clean and you'll get your babies.

And *they* will be safe and clean.

But if you don't do what I say I will make this house fall to pieces.

So do as you're told.

Be my friend.

And it will be so easy for you.

Like jam down my throat.

> *(The sound of knocking on glass.)*

And I can make this house fall apart, June.

Don't think I can't.

> *(Rain.)*

> *(The knocking continues.)*

> *(A shadow at the back door.)*

LEROY. *(From the other side of the kitchen door.)* Lurie? June? Anybody home? Your company all gone?

> *(Thunder.)*

I'm here to fix the floor.

> *(More knocking.)*

What you need to do is give a brother a key.

> (**BEATRICE** *enters, towel on her head, in a bathrobe.*)

> (*More knocking.*)

BEATRICE. Grrrr.

LEROY. Damn, man –

> (*Thunder.*)

> (*The shadow retreats.*)

> (**BEATRICE** *seems a bit unsteady on her feet.*)

> (*Tinny music box notes...*)

> (**BEATRICE** *bangs her head with her hand.*)

> (*She moans.*)

> (*The music stops.*)

BEATRICE. Better.

> (*The rain quiets.*)

Much better.

> (*She pats her stomach, goes to the cupboard.*)

> (*Empty.*)

Grrrr.

> (*She calls out.*)

I am not about to start eating bread and margarine.
Who's going to fix this?

...

BEATRICE. My stomach hurts and I'm hungry.

> ...

> *I said my stomach hurts and I'm hungry.*

>> *(The house rattles.)*

>> *(JUNE enters.)*

JUNE. Don't break anything.

BEATRICE. I need jam.

JUNE. I have to make more.

BEATRICE. Well you'd better hurry.

JUNE. It takes time.

BEATRICE. Well you should have started way before now.

> When I was first started running low.

> I need a lot. Now I'm awfully hungry and I.

> I'm not quite myself.

>> *(She yawns.)*

>> *(JUNE begins to make jam.)*

> You'll do my hair next.

> Ringlets all over my head just like Shirley.

> Shirley's mother made a curl right above her eyebrow to hide a scar.

> So I'd like a curl right above my eyebrow, please. Of course.

> *What are you doing?*

JUNE. Boiling the jars. Sterilizing them.

BEATRICE. Ahhh. The jam will be most clean because the jars will be most clean.

Very good idea, June.

Because that will help me be most clean, too.

I'm thirsty.

I said, I'm *thirsty*.

JUNE. Milk?

BEATRICE. Growing girls need lots of milk. It's what helps them leave their girl days behind.

You're helping me so much with this milk. And that jam.

When I taste these I know exactly who I am and who I am not.

I am not wicked. I have not seen the nakedness of –.

Let's dance like we used to.

JUNE. I'm making jam.

BEATRICE. Then I'll dance. I'll dance for you. You'll like it, you'll see.

> *(She climbs onto the table and begins to tap dance.)*

K-K-K-KATY, BEAUTIFUL KATY
YOU'RE THE ONLY G-G-G-GIRL
THAT I ADORE
WHEN THE M-M-M-MOON SHINES
OVER THE MOUNTAIN
I'LL BE WAITING BY THE K-K-K KITCHEN DOOR.

> (**BEATRICE** *waits for applause.*)

...

> *(She starts again.)*

K-K-K-KATY, BEAUTIFUL KATY
YOU'RE THE ONLY G-G-G-GIRL

BEATRICE.
THAT I ADORE
WHEN THE M-M-M-MOON SHINES
OVER THE MOUNTAIN
I'LL BE WAITING BY THE K-K-K KITCHEN DOOR.

(As she dances, JUNE continues to make jam.)

(JUNE watches BEATRICE, then deliberately turns on the faucet.)

(Whiiiiiiinnnne.)

(Pipes.)

(A music box. Tinny.)
K-K-K KATY...

(BEATRICE clutches her head.)

Stop, stop, stop.

(The house rattles. The pipes whine.)

Theysawnottheirfather'snakedness.Theysawnottheir father'snakedness.

Theysawnottheirfather'snakedness...

(BEATRICE curls into a ball on the table.)

(JUNE turns the faucet off.)

(JUNE waits.)

(Waits.)

(But BEATRICE is still alive.)

Do...do my hair next?

All over my head?

Pin curls.

Over one.

Eyebrow.

>(**BEATRICE** *does not move, though.*)

>(**JUNE** *pulls* **BEATRICE**'s *hair back, as if she might be about to begin...*)

>(**BEATRICE** *falls asleep.*)

>(**JUNE** *grips* **BEATRICE**'s *hair. It is not nice.*)

>(*Then.*)

I can feel the pit of my stomach.

>(*Then back to sleep.*)

>(*Dark.*)

>(*Scrape, scrape, scrape.*)

>(*Digging, digging.*)

>(*A shadow at the kitchen door.*)

>(*Lights.*)

>(*The bathroom.*)

>(**JUNE** *digging.*)

JUNE. My house—my house—my house...

>(*Dark.*)

>(*Lights.*)

>(*The kitchen.*)

(**BEATRICE** *on the table, same as before.*)

(**LURIE** *approaches, unsure...*)

BEATRICE. I can feel the pit of my stomach, Lurie. It hurts. When I close my eyes and listen very hard I can hear it rumbling. A little gurgle. A little brook bubbling inside.

(*She yawns.*)

I need more jam.

LURIE. June's –

BEATRICE. Not fast enough. You're supposed to feed me when I want. Both of you. Where *is* June?

LURIE. Fixing the floor.

BEATRICE. I hope.

LURIE. The way you want. LeRoy was supposed to come –

BEATRICE. I don't think he's up to snuff, Lurie.

LURIE. Was he here? He can help.

BEATRICE. Forget about him. *We're* friends now. *We're* practically family now.

LURIE. Did you?

Do...do something to him?

(**BEATRICE** *bangs a hand on the table.*)

BEATRICE. FORGET EVERTHING ABOUT HIM.

I said no. No no no. It is just us. The way it should be. Shirley and her friends.

One movie has Shirley dressed in little hoop skirts and ruffly pants undernearth.

Those skirts bounced right along while she tapped. A very lovely old black man danced with her.

LURIE. Bo Jangles.

BEATRICE. Well how am I supposed to remember his name?

LURIE. That's his name.

BEATRICE. All for Shirley.

LURIE. I'll go get June.

BEATRICE. You know what will make me feel better?

LURIE. I'll go get June.

BEATRICE. Is if you be Bo what's his name, and I be Shirley in her hoop skirt.

LURIE. You said only June should dance with you.

BEATRICE. Something is going very wrong, Lurie. I can hardly stand. This. This will make me feel better.

LURIE. Last time you brought up dancing you twisted everything around. You made it look like I –

BEATRICE. I'm only asking to be polite. You and I both know, Lurie, that I don't have to ask at all. If you really want this house. If you really want June and those babies, you'll do it and you know it.

> (*Scraping, digging...* **JUNE***...*)

> (*The bathroom.*)

JUNE. Mine-mine-mine-and *you-are-going-back.*

> (*The kitchen.*)

BEATRICE. Do you really want those babies?

Because if you really want those babies you'd better think of a dance real quick.

It can take place anywhere.

In the movie Shirley's name was Virgie.

BEATRICE. And Virgie had that Uncle Billy friend and he'd do just *anything* for her.

And bad men kept trying to come down to where they lived and ruin everything,

But in the end Virgie and her uncle Billy save the day.

It can be like that.

LURIE. No, I'll get June –

BEATRICE. June has caused enough trouble, forgetting to make my jam, starving me half to death.

Deep, deep down you can, I know you can. Deep, deep down is where some of our best feelings are. And, pretending can be great fun. Deep, deep down you can pretend anything you want.

LURIE. I don't want to pretend that.

BEATRICE. Deep, deep down you can be as firm as you like, or as nice as you like.

You can use the teeth God gave you,

Instead of sucking down bread and margarine,

Instead of worrying about contractors, and sprinkler system men and plumbers.

Deep down there's no Bill Blake, there's no June even.

You are a true friend Lurie.

My best friend.

You will feel most alive, ever, ever, ever, doing this.

I promise.

> *(Dark.)*

> *(Then: the bathroom.)*

(**JUNE** *stands over a hole in the bathroom floor.*)

JUNE. Mine.

(*The kitchen.*)

(**LURIE** *and* **BEATRICE** *poised for a dance – Shirley Temple/Bo Jangles style.*)

(*They dance.*)

(*They dance off the tables and through the kitchen.*)

(*When they dance past* **JUNE**, *she holds out her hands for a dance with* **LURIE**. **LURIE** *and* **JUNE** *dance, and* **BEATRICE** *is excited. She wants to join, too. She holds her hands out to* **JUNE**, *who takes them.*)

(*Newspaper blows around the three of them.*)

(*Tango music*.*)

(**BEATRICE** *and* **JUNE** *Tango.* **JUNE***'s dancing is rough and quick and* **BEATRICE** *struggles to keep up. The house groans. Finally,* **BEATRICE** *pulls away, exhausted. She crumbles to the floor.*)

(*Knocking can be heard.*)

BEATRICE. I'm very hungry, so hungry.

JUNE & LURIE. ...

---

* A license to produce *Feeding Beatrice* does not include a performance license for any third-party or copyrighted music. Licensees should create an original composition or use music in the public domain. For further information, please see the Music and Third Party Materials Use Note on page iii.

BEATRICE. Feed me, I said I'm hungry.

JUNE. It's not ready yet.

BEATRICE. The pit of my stomach hurts, Lurie. Tell her... tell her...deep, deep... June's trying to hurt me. Just like *she* did that day, my last day, the day she sealed me up.

> *(Quiet, quiet, then...)*

She'd seen me.

Looking down at my stomach, the pit of my stomach,

Which should have been empty,

But she knew it was not empty.

She knew it was full with something that was very wrong.

I was sitting on the rim, just balancing of the rim of that bathtub over there.

My music box was playing.

I set it right up on the floor over there so I could listen to it.

And the faucet was running.

The sound of the hot water pipes was very sharp, so sharp.

My father was supposed to have that fixed.

She was always after him to have that fixed.

"Fix those pipes, this isn't the country, this isn't Mississippi, this isn't Arkansas.

For Pete's sake."

And as I reached to turn off the faucet I saw her in the doorway, in the corner of my eye.

"This isn't Mississippi, this isn't Arkansas."

BEATRICE. And then her hands around my neck

and then sound of that music box

and the faucet still shrieking

and her elbows sloshing that water

while she squeezed my throat

and my head hitting the tub.

And then just black.

Theysawnottheirfather'swickedness.Theysawnottheir father'swickedness.

So you see.

How I needed someone to be clean against.

My wicked parts were my only company for so long.

I've been choking on my own dusty filth for so long.

Until you came and began to clear it all away.

Light shone down on me, enough for even Jesus to see.

Enough to dry my wicked parts into shriveled crisps.

For the first time I was very big, very strong.

I liked that very much.

Please, feed me.

(But **JUNE** *and* **LURIE** *just stand. And watch.)*

Dance for me. Talk to me. Anything. Anything at all.

(But **JUNE** *and* **LURIE** *just stand. And watch.)*

Theysawnottheirfather'swickedness.Theysawnottheir father'swickedness.

(Her voice gets softer and softer.)

(It is about to disappear.)

BEATRICE. Then dust. For so long.

> *(The house quiets.)*

> *(**BEATRICE** is still.)*

> *(**JUNE** nudges her.)*

> *(**LURIE** nudges her.)*

> *(**BEATRICE** takes one last long shudder.)*

> *(**JUNE** and **LURIE** jump back.)*

JUNE & LURIE. Ahhh.

> *(But then: nothing.)*

> *(Quiet.)*

LURIE. What should we –?

> *(**JUNE** pushed **BEATRICE** back into the hole and covers her up with tile.)*

We did it. We sealed her up. We're okay. She's gone. We can live here now. *We can live here now.*

> *(**LURIE** hugs **JUNE**.)*

> *(**LURIE** kisses **JUNE**.)*

JUNE. I. Me.

LURIE. She's gone.

JUNE. *I* sealed her up.

LURIE. But she's *gone*. Baby, she's *gone*.

JUNE. How did it feel?

LURIE. Baby?

JUNE. How did it *feel*?

LURIE. June.

JUNE. Dancing around like some kind of –

LURIE. No.No, / no, no. June.

JUNE. Jim Crow.

LURIE. Come on, now –

JUNE. – some kind of Jim Crow yes massa, shufflin' and a singin' –

LURIE. We wanted this house.

JUNE. With *us* in it. Not, not, not whoever that was sidling up to that girl like, like –

LURIE. The house. The house is ours now.

JUNE. What kind of father could you be if somewhere that's a part of you, for all to see?

LURIE. I was *doing* it for *us*.

JUNE. You push that part down, Lurie, you do not let it, let it rise up and out.

LURIE. I did that for *you*. For us. For birthdays and Christmases. So our kids can run *upstairs* and *downstairs*...

(The shadow at the kitchen door.)

JUNE. Get out of my house.

(Knocking.)

LURIE. It wasn't just me. You were getting jam and towels like you were some prized mammy –

JUNE. You don't love this house.

LURIE. I don't love this house?

JUNE. You would have left it if you could. A million times you've said so.

LURIE. I was earning this house. We were earning this house. Together. Like we agreed.

We deserve this house. We've waited so long. We're good people and we saved and waited and we deserve good things like everyone else and we shouldn't have to fight so hard to live in here together. We fed ourselves this house and it almost swallowed us whole. It almost left us half chewed on the floor but we made it we did it we're both still here.

> (**LURIE** *embraces* **JUNE**.)

June.

I love you.

> (**JUNE** *resists but* **LURIE** *hugs her harder.*)

I love you and I love this house. I love you and I love this house.

> (**LURIE** *squeezes* **JUNE** *hard.*)

I love you. I love you. I love you.

> (*They struggle.* **JUNE** *tries to break free but can't. Finally,* **JUNE** *goes limp and* **LURIE** *eases his hold on* **JUNE** *just enough for* **JUNE** *to regain herself, reach for the hammer on the floor, and swing it at* **LURIE***'s head. The hammer hits* **LURIE** *hard.* **LURIE** *falls.* **JUNE** *stands over* **LURIE***, but* **LURIE** *does not move.*)

> (**JUNE** *uses the hammer to begin digging another hole in the floor.*)

JUNE. All mine.

> (*The tinny house of the music box.*)

> (*Knocking.*)

(The shadow at the kitchen door.)

LEROY. You all home? I'm gonna fix that floor.

*(**JUNE** stands over **LURIE**, hammer in hand.)*

*(**LURIE** looks up at **JUNE**.)*

(Creeeeaaaaak.)

(Blackout.)

End of Play